"Get out of here!"
Lyn cried, sobbing

Her breathing uneven, Lyn looked up at him as she spoke.

Beric stared long at her, then turned abruptly and walked out.

Lyn leaned back against the cool wall, eyes shut, feeling sick inside. Had she ruined all her carefully made plans because she'd got angry when he touched her? She remembered the feel of his hands on her body and trembled with desire.

Slowly she gathered up her things and hesitated by the door, not knowing how to go out there and face him. Then she recalled the way she'd felt the day she was taken to prison. This ordeal was nothing compared to that.

Purposely Lyn squared her shoulders and walked out into the sun where Beric, the man she'd once loved, waited....

D0040741

SALLY WENTWORTH
is also the author of these

Harlequin Presents

and these

Harlequin Romances

SALLY WENTWORTH

the judas kiss

Harlequin Books

TORONTO · LONDON · LOS ANGELES · AMSTERDAM
SYDNEY · HAMBURG · PARIS · STOCKHOLM · ATHENS · TOKYO

Harlequin Presents edition published January 1982
ISBN 0-373-10480-4

Original hardcover edition published in 1981
by Mills & Boon Limited

CHAPTER ONE

THE man and the girl were locked together in a close embrace. They stood on the edge of the moonlit, deserted beach in the deep shadow of a palm tree, its fronds moving slightly in the night breeze and casting dappled patterns over their still figures. But they were oblivious of their surroundings, as unaware of the soft pounding of the ocean waves upon the long white beach as of the brightly lit towers of the resort hotels behind them. They were lost to everything but their own desire, the urgent passion of their kiss and the closeness of their bodies as they clung together.

It was the sound of laughter and singing that disturbed them. The man looked up and saw a group of white-clad women making their way down through the hotel grounds, past the swimming pool and on to the beach about thirty yards along. The women were members of a religious convention staying at the hotel and they gathered near the water's edge and began to sing hymns, their bodies moving from side to side in time with the music, gently clapping their hands.

The man looked down to where the girl nestled her head against his shoulder, her long-lashed eyes closed, her breathing still uneven. Gently he ran his finger down her nose, over its rather high bridge and down to her lips. 'Hey, have you gone to sleep?'

She smiled a little and tried to catch his finger between her teeth, then opened her eyes to look up at him, soft brown eyes still dark with desire and lit with

5

an inner glow of happiness. 'No, I'm not asleep. I don't want to go to sleep tonight.'

'Not even to dream of me?' he asked teasingly.

She reached up to put her arms round his neck. 'I'd rather be awake and here with you. Oh, Beric . . .' She lifted up her face, lips parted sensuously, and he kissed her again hungrily, feeling her mouth open eagerly under his, warm and responsive.

'Lyn.' He breathed her name hoarsely as she moved against him, the urgency in her own body creating an almost uncontrollable need in his. Catching hold of her shoulders, he pushed her almost roughly away, his hands shaking, his breathing ragged. 'For God's sake, Lyn, if you only knew what you're doing to me!'

A spark of mischief lit her eyes and she tried to move her hips near him again, but he held her off. 'Why, what am I doing to you?'

Beric smiled down at her, an amused curve to his lips, knowing that she was trying out her powers over him. He wound his hand among her mass of dark brown curls and pulled gently. 'Driving me mad, of course. Behave yourself, you little minx, or I won't be answerable for the consequences.'

Lyn's eyes grew serious and she put up her hands to rest them on his chest. Huskily, not looking at him, she said, 'Maybe I—I might like it if you weren't answerable—might like the consequences, I mean.' Uncertainly she raised her eyes to look at him.

'Darling!' He pulled her close and kissed her forehead, delighting in her innocence, his heart stirred by the inexperienced way in which she had tried to tell him; afraid to betray too much of her feelings for fear of a rebuff and yet determined to let him know that she wanted him. 'There's plenty of time, we don't have to rush into anything. We've only known each other a few weeks. And you're so young . . .'

Restlessly Lyn moved in his arms. 'No, I'm not. I'm nineteen. Plenty old enough to . . .' She flushed. 'There are lots of girls my age in the Airline who . . .'

'Who sleep around?' he finished for her, his mouth contemptuous. 'Is that what you're trying to say?' he demanded bluntly. 'Sure there are. Most of the stewardesses have been going to bed with men from the moment they left home. They look upon themselves as liberated career women and expect to sleep with any man they fancy, even after only a first date. And it isn't only stewardesses; you've seen the girls who hang around the hotels where the aircrews stay during lay-overs, they're always on the lookout for pilots. Seem to think that because they wear a uniform and belong to a so-called glamorous profession it turns them into some kind of a stud.'

'And are you saying that you've never taken advantage of all these offers?' Lyn demanded tartly.

His hands tightened angrily on her arms. 'No, I'm not,' he bit back bluntly. 'My sex drive is as normal as the next man's, and when a good-looking girl throws herself at my head I've been known to take her up on the offer. But those kind of girls are only good for one-night stands; I sure as hell wouldn't want to break any of my rules for them.'

'Your—rules?'

'Yes, you brainless idiot. The rules that say don't get involved, never get serious about a stewardess, and that no woman is worth losing your freedom for. Those kind of rules—the ones that bachelor pilots swear by.

Until the right kind of girl eventually comes along, that is. A girl with innocence in her face and real warmth in her eyes. Who doesn't know how to hide her feelings and who doesn't turn them on and off like a tap.'

'Oh.' Lyn looked up at the lean handsomeness of his features with a bemused look on her face. 'Do you—do you mean *me*?'

He grinned down at her. 'Yes, you lovely nut, of course I mean you.' He put his hands on both sides of her face and looked at her earnestly. 'But, as I said, Lyn, we have plenty of time. I don't want to rush things and spoil what we've got going for us. Let's take it nice and easy, okay?'

Gently she pulled his hands away and smiled mistily up at him. 'Okay, but it won't be easy. Not if you go on kissing me like that.'

Beric laughed and put his arm round her waist. 'I seem to remember you were doing your share of the kissing.'

Lyn frowned. '*Was* I? I really can't recall . . .'

He laughed again, a full masculine laugh of enjoyment. 'In that case I shall just have to remind you . . .' and he swung her round to hold her close and kiss her again.

Eventually, he reluctantly let her go and said unevenly, 'We are *definitely* going back to the hotel. We've an early flight tomorrow, don't forget.'

'Mmm.' Lyn leant her head contentedly against his shoulder and let him lead her back through the grounds towards the main building.

The poolside bar where they sold exotic rum-based drinks at even more exotic prices was closing and the last customers noisily leaving, not very many of them, because it was the off-season in Miami Beach, the temperatures too hot for the average visitor. Even now, at eleven at night, it was still eighty-six degrees Fahrenheit, warm enough for Lyn to wear just a thin cotton sundress and Beric a short-sleeved casual shirt worn loose over lightweight trousers. They sauntered past the empty pool with rows of sun-loungers set round its edge under the shade of the palms, past the whirlpool Jacuzzi baths and under the false hill of rock where there was a tiny shop selling imitation pearl and coral jewellery and a seafood bar. But these were closed up now and there was only the noise of the continuous flow of water pumped up to the top of the hill and falling in a mock waterfall back into the pool for the delight of the swimmers who flocked there during the day.

As they neared the hotel they could hear music emanating from the night-club on the first floor, a girl singer putting everything she'd got and then some into one of the hottest chart-topping numbers. Lyn remembered hearing it on the radio, the lyric heavy with sexual overtones that had left little to the imagination. The night-club, the song—they all seemed a world away from the moonlit, scented gardens, from the wonderful thing that was happening between the two of them. Something that as yet was still too new for her to fully comprehend, to really believe would go on growing into a lasting relationship. Even now, she felt as if she ought to pinch herself to make sure she wasn't in the middle of a fantastic dream, that she was really here in Miami with Beric's arm round her, her head resting against his shoulder as they walked.

It had all happened so quickly, she could hardly believe that it was only a few months ago that she had eventually managed to overcome the opposition of her rather staid, old-fashioned parents and applied for a job as a stewardess with Air International. The interview had been nerve-racking, but then had come the exciting day when she had received a letter of acceptance, followed by several weeks at the training school where she had joined a group of other young women *and men*—for this was no longer a completely female-dominated profession—in learning the thousand and one tasks that went into making an air steward or stewardess.

Then had come a few weeks of getting used to the job on shorter, European flights, where Lyn had expected to stay for some time, but because of expansion by the company on to new routes, which coincided with the increase in holiday traffic to the United States, she had been given the incredible news that she was going to be put on to the Miami run. Lyn could hardly believe her luck; the transatlantic routes were the most coveted in the airline, giving the crews the chance to soak up the sun in two or three-day lay-overs in Miami. The pilots, too, were usually younger and tended to be more sociable than on shorter flights, so most of the unattached personnel were keen to get on the route.

Beric had been on her very first transatlantic flight. The Chief Stewardess had taken her under her wing at Heathrow Airport and introduced her to the other cabin staff and then led her along to meet the rest of the crew. Lyn saw the three men walking towards her and swallowed; even now she found the senior officers rather intimidating. The Captain shook her hand, welcomed her to his flight, and turned to introduce her to the other two men: the Flight Engineer who gave her a friendly smile and made a joke about her newness, and then Beric, very tall and handsome in the dark uniform with the three gold stripes of a Senior First Officer on his sleeve, his eyes of an incredible blue running over her in cool appraisal. He nodded to her, his lips curling into a slow smile, and shook hands. Lyn stared at him, feeling completely devastated, never having met anyone with such clean-cut good looks before. He was tall, dark, tanned and gorgeous. She felt the pressure of his hand on hers and, like a complete fool, felt her cheeks suffuse with colour. A look of utter disbelief came into Beric's eyes, to be followed by one of arrested surprise as she quickly disengaged her hand and hurried away, feeling that she'd made an idiot of herself.

But it was that blush that had first aroused Beric's interest and had made him, one of the most sought-after bachelors on the airline, seek her out and ask her for a date. At first she had been nervous and very much in awe of him, expecting him to find her gauche and inexperienced, and thought he would soon drop her for one of the more sophisticated girls. But he had been very patient, taking pains to put her at her ease, and soon she had begun to gain confidence and to be her usual sparkling self, full of fun and love of life, her warmth and vivaciousness shining in her brown eyes. Why he singled her out Lyn didn't know; she was tall and her figure was okay, but no one could describe her as beautiful; the bump in her nose put paid to that. But Beric would run his finger down it when she complained and say he liked it, it was aristocratic, and she was content, incredibly thanking her guardian angel for the sheer happiness of being with him.

They had been dating for about six weeks now, six wonderful weeks in which Beric had awakened a passionate side of her nature that had been completely dormant before. When she was with him she seemed to come alive, to sparkle with radiant happiness, and when she was away from him for any length of time she felt as if the world was flat and empty, longed to be with him again and could think of nothing else but him all day long. She had—as one of her fellow stewardesses described it—got it badly, but Lyn didn't care; for the first time in her young life she had fallen head over heels in love, and it was the most fantastic feeling in the world.

Beric had kissed her often, of course, but he had always been fully in control, not letting things become too serious, but his kisses aroused such fires in her that soon Lyn wanted more, much more. She clung to him, feeling the hardness of his body against her own, and moved against him, unwittingly quickening his own passions. But always he had drawn back, leaving her for a while feeling frustrated and unfulfilled until the sheer happiness of being in love took over again.

Now they walked slowly towards the hotel, stopping for a last kiss before going through the garden entrance and strolling between the basement shopping arcade towards the lifts. As this was America, the shops were still open even this late: a couple of chic clothing boutiques, a camera shop, drugstore, florist, and toyshop. The window of this last one was full of the most gorgeous toys. Beric glanced into it as they passed, then suddenly stopped and said, 'Wait here. I won't be more than a minute.'

Lyn looked after him with a rather mystified face, but obediently did as she was told, amusing herself by watching all the children playing with the electronic video games in the room across the corridor, their heads bent as they stared at the screens in engrossed concentration. Then Beric came out of the shop and she forgot everything else as she gave an exclamation of delighted surprise. In his arms, almost obscuring him from view, he carried a huge furry white panda bear, with black ears and the most wistful black eyes.

He looked round it and grinned at her. 'Here,' he said, holding the bear out to her, 'this is for you to cuddle in bed—until you get a permanent replacement!'

Lyn took the bear from him and looked at it in delight. 'Oh, he's gorgeous!' She gave the toy a hug. 'Mmm, and *very* cuddly.' Raising her eyes, she looked at Beric mischievously. 'So cuddly that I may not *want* to replace him.'

Beric immediately made a grab at the bear. 'In that case I'll take him back.'

'No!' Lyn moved quickly away. 'He's mine now. And I love him.' Her face became a little shy as she added, using the endearment for the first time, 'Thank you, darling.'

Beric didn't say anything, but his eyes, so unbelievably blue, took on a new warmth as he put a protective arm across her shoulders and led her towards the lifts.

At her door, he gave her only a brief kiss on the forehead before warning her to ask for an early wake-up call, and she didn't see him again until they met at Miami Airport the next morning just before boarding the plane. The whole crew were there and she was being teased unmercifully about the panda bear. The Captain was trying to keep a serious face as he told her it was so big that she would definitely have to pay full fare for it, and the Chief Stewardess was saying that all animals had to be carried in the cargo hold. Lyn laughed at them and turned a glowing face to Beric. He moved towards her, but as he did so one of the other stewardesses stepped past him. She stumbled, and in the confusion Lyn's tote bag was knocked over, spilling the contents all over the floor. Beric, the stewardess and several of the others goodnaturedly bent to help Lyn pick the things up, stuffing make-up, toiletries, her purse, passport and everything else back in the bag.

Beric stood up and handed it to her: 'I never knew a woman to carry so much stuff around.' But he grinned when he said it and her heart gave a great lurch of love, all mixed up with longing and pride.

The flight back to England was uneventful; hard work as usual coping with all the passengers on the long flight, but there were a couple of hours in which the cabin crew could relax while the films were being shown. Lyn took the opportunity to freshen up, pushing aside the disordered contents of her bag as she searched for her comb and lipstick. She started to tidy the things, but then a man came along asking for a blanket for his wife who was trying to sleep and the other stewardess asked her to get it. After that she seemed to be kept busy the rest of the way and gave a tired sigh of relief when at last they landed and had seen off all the passengers and checked the plane for anything that had been left behind.

Beric waited for her as they walked in a group towards Customs, Lyn clutching her panda and trying to find her passport in her bag at the same time.

'Here, you'd better let me take that.' He took her bag from her and paused while he looked for her passport.

Lyn walked a little way ahead, but he soon caught

her up and handed her the passport and helped her put the strap of her bag on her shoulder. She tried to stifle a yawn and he laughed. 'I bet right now you're cursing the person who told you flying was a glamour job!'

'It's all right for you—you get to fly sitting down,' she quipped as she smiled happily back at him, her brown eyes a mirror of her emotions.

At the Customs desk there was a hold-up and one of the stewards groaned. 'Oh, no! They're doing one of their spot checks. I suppose that means we'll all be taken to be searched. And I wanted to get home early today, too. Isn't it always the way?' he remarked to no one in particular, his voice heavy with disgust.

It was the first time that Lyn had ever been submitted to an intensive Customs check, but the other girls all accepted it philosophically as part of the job, handing over their bags and going resignedly off with one of the female Customs officers. Lyn didn't like the body search but submitted to it, eager to get it over so that she could rejoin Beric and discuss where they would spend the evening. After her search she was allowed to dress again, but was kept waiting for a long time before the female officer came back with another male officer. He was carrying her passport in his hand.

Glancing down at it, he said, 'Miss Lynette Maxwell?'

'Yes.'

'I wonder if you'd mind accompanying me to my office for a few moments?'

Mystified, Lyn nodded and walked out of the little search room. The two closed in on either side of her, hemming her in.

'This way.' The man led her a short way down an

empty corridor and opened the door into a much larger office with a big black table in its centre. On the table was spread the entire contents of her tote bag and there were several other Customs men carefully taking everything apart: her lipstick, address book, toothpaste tube—everything. But Lyn's stupefied gaze had no sooner taken this in than she realised that an even worse horror was being perpetrated. Over in the corner a man had put her panda bear on another table and had picked up a knife.

Lyn gave a cry of shock and dismay and made an impulsive movement to try and stop him, but immediately her arms were grabbed by her two escorts and she was held back. She looked up at the man appealingly. 'But you can't! Please!'

He returned her gaze coldly, then nodded to the man in the corner. The knife came down and slit through the soft roundness of the bear's white stomach. He put his hand inside and methodically began to shred through the stuffing.

Lyn looked away, tears close to her eyes, and turned angrily on the Customs officer beside her who seemed to be in charge. 'How *dare* you?' she demanded. 'You have no right to do that!'

Heavily he answered, 'I assure you, Miss Maxwell, that we have full powers to examine every article brought into this country if we have cause for our suspicions to be aroused.'

'Well, you haven't,' Lyn retorted. 'That bear was a present to me. It was only given to me last night. Oh, please, tell him to stop!'

But the man merely gestured to all her things on the table. 'This is your bag, Miss Maxwell?'

'What? Oh, yes.'

'And these articles all belong to you?'

'If they came out of my bag, yes.' Lyn stopped, looking around her at the grim faces of the Customs people, realising for the first time that there was something seriously wrong. Her anger giving way to fear, she said nervously, 'I—I don't understand. Why are you doing this?'

Slowly the man reached down and with a pair of tweezers picked up a carton of talcum powder. Its lid had been prized off and the contents emptied on to a sheet of clear plastic. 'This is your talcum powder?'

Lyn looked at the carton rather dazedly. 'Yes, I think so.' She tried to pull herself together, and looked more closely, then shook her head. 'Why, no, I don't think it is. I bought a new carton in Miami, but I don't think it was that brand.' A puzzled frown on her brow, she looked up at her questioner. 'Why? Won't you please tell me what's happening?'

He carefully put the carton down again and said, without any trace of emotion, 'This carton was found to contain pure heroin. It is now my duty to hand you over to the local police who will charge you with smuggling narcotics into the country.'

Her face white with appalled horror and shock, Lyn could only stammer, 'But—but I didn't! I didn't, I tell you!'

The man's eyes grew cold. 'In that case, Miss Maxwell, you have nothing to be afraid of, have you? All you have to do is convince the police that a carton of heroin worth a great deal of money somehow found its own way into your bag.'

Lyn stared at him, her face ashen, then slowly sat down on a chair as she watched them go through the rest of her things.

She sat there for a long time. At some point a detective sergeant from the local police station arrived, but Lyn hardly noticed. She felt a strange kind of numbness, as if this couldn't really be happening to her, that it must be some kind of very vivid nightmare from which she would soon wake. Eventually, when they'd gone through everything, the sergeant came over and told her that he was arresting her and she would have to accompany him to the police station. Vaguely, in the back of her mind, Lyn heard him speaking, but her eyes were fixed on the remnants of her panda bear, lying in a pathetic heap of black and white fur and stuffing, on the floor at the Customs man's feet.

A woman police constable put a hand on her arm and Lyn looked up at her vacantly. Slowly she got to her feet and allowed herself to be led out of the office, the sergeant and another policeman close behind her. They had to go past the counters where all the airline crews checked in. A Swissair flight had just come in and were passing through normally without any close checks or body searches, the Customs men looking their usual bored selves. Several people turned to look at them as they passed and Lyn lifted her chin bravely, but kept her face averted.

Then she saw Beric; he was waiting at the end of the room, leaning negligently against one of the empty counters, jacket open, cap pushed back on his head and smoking a cigarette. There had been time to smoke a whole packet while he'd been waiting. He saw her and straightened up, his eyes taking in her escort and realising at once what had happened. Lyn gave a sudden convulsive movement that shook off the restraining hands and ran to throw herself in Beric's arms.

He threw down the cigarette and held her close. The policemen rushed up and tried to pull her away, but he didn't let go.

'Oh, Beric, they said I had dope in my bag. Tell them I didn't do it. Oh, please, *please* tell them I didn't do it!' She turned her scared, anxious face up to him and burst into frightened tears, the knowledge that it was all too horrifyingly real finally hitting home.

The sergeant spoke sharply. 'Let her go! Miss Maxwell is under arrest.'

Beric's arms tightened and Lyn clung to him desperately. *This* was real, the feel of his strength encompassing her, the overwhelming relief of knowing that she had someone to stand by her and help her. Someone to protect her from this terrible thing that had happened to her.

Above her head, Beric said grimly, 'In that case I insist on going with her.'

The sergeant's glance ran over him, taking in his size and the determination in the blue eyes. Suspiciously he said, 'And who might you be?' adding, 'Sir,' after a deliberate pause to let Beric know that he was the one with all the power in this situation.

Beric got the message but couldn't have cared less. Coldly he answered, 'The name's Beric Dane. I'm the First Officer on Miss Maxwell's flight.'

Realising that he wasn't to be intimidated, the sergeant nodded. 'Very well. We're taking Miss Maxwell to the local station.'

They let her sit next to him in the back of the police car and he kept his arm tightly round her, putting up his other hand to gently wipe away her tears. Lyn tried to smile at him, but couldn't, and buried her head in his shoulder. He kissed her forehead and gently stroked her hair, but neither of them spoke. Somehow it would have seemed profane to speak endearments with the inimical ears of the police listening in.

At the station she was taken away and Beric was left to wait again. She was formally charged and had to have her fingerprints taken, then she was asked a lot of questions for a long time. Who had given her the heroin? How was she supposed to pass it on? How much had she been paid? The questions seemed to go on endlessly, but she could only repeat the truth; that the carton of talcum powder wasn't hers and she didn't know how it had got into her bag. In the end they let her make a statement to that effect and while it was being typed she was allowed to see Beric again.

For a few moments they clung together, then he kissed her hard on the mouth, his hands on either side of her face.

'Don't worry,' he told her roughly, his own face taut as he saw the fear and agony in hers. 'I know you didn't do it. I'm going to get you a good lawyer and we'll have you out of here in no time. Then all we'll have to do is find out who planted the stuff on you.'

Lyn stared at him wide-eyed. 'You think that's what happened? That someone deliberately planted it in my bag to get me into trouble?'

He shook his head. 'Not you specially, no. From the way that we were all searched it seems likely that the Customs were given a tip-off, told that someone on our flight would be trying to smuggle the stuff in. And whoever it was must have got some idea of what was happening and decided to offload the stuff on to someone else.'

'And I just happened to be the victim?' Lyn said bitterly.

Beric grinned. 'Probably thought you looked the most innocent,' he said teasingly, trying to cheer her, and lifted a finger to lightly trace the outline of her lips.

Lyn kissed his finger but couldn't manage a smile. 'But what about when we got through the Customs?' she objected. 'How would they have got it back?'

He shrugged. 'Made some excuse, perhaps, if it was one of the girls. Say hers could have got mixed up with yours back at the hotel.'

'One of the girls?' Lyn stared at him. 'But surely you don't think . . .'

'I don't know,' he interrupted her swiftly. 'But people do crazy things when they get addicted to drugs—or money, if it comes to that. It might not even have been one of the crew, it could have been a pas senger. For all we know everyone on that flight might have been searched.'

Lyn looked up at him despairingly. 'Then how will we ever find out who put it there?'

Putting his hands on her shoulders, he squeezed them reassuringly. 'If the stuff wasn't yours it won't have your prints on it, but whoever the swine was who put it in your bag must have left his fingerprints, we only have to find out whose they are and bingo—we're home and dry!'

'Oh, Beric, do you really think so?' This time she did manage a smile, for the first time seeing some gleam of hope in this whole horrible mess.

'It may take some time, mind,' he warned her. 'Don't expect miracles. Obviously whoever did it is trying to get as far away from here as possible—and Heathrow Airport is just the place to do it,' he added wryly. But seeing the immediate fear that came back into her eyes, he went on quickly, 'But no matter how long it takes we're going to find him and clear your name.' He looked at her earnestly. 'Do you believe that, Lyn? Do you?'

She nodded, her eyes fixed on his face, drawing from it the strength and courage she needed. 'Yes, I believe it. So long as I have you,' she said huskily.

'We'll fight it together.' He smiled and playfully bunched his fist to punch her on the jaw. 'All my muscle is at your disposal, ma'am.'

Lyn caught his hand and opened it, twined her fingers in his. 'Oh, Beric, I'm so afraid. How long will I have to stay here?'

'No longer than it takes me to get a lawyer and to fix bail for you. I swear it. Now, how about your parents? You'd better give me their address so that I can let them know what's happened and where you are. Is there anyone else you want me to notify?'

She shook her head. 'No, I don't think so.'

He wrote her parents' address down in a notebook and then said slowly, 'Lyn, you'll have to face the fact that you might have to stay here overnight. You'll have to appear at a magistrates' court tomorrow and bail may not be set until then.'

'Stay here tonight? You mean in a cell? Oh, Beric, no! I can't!' Tears came to her eyes again and she clung to him fiercely. 'I tell you I can't!'

'Hey there, where's my brave girl gone?' Gently he pushed her away, holding on to her arms. 'It's only maybe—and only for a night even then. Come on, you can take it.' Gently he stroked her face and Lyn gave a little tremor of sensuality. Even now, in these circumstances, the touch of his hand against her skin could rouse her sexually.

He kissed her gently, lingeringly, then said, 'I must leave you now, Lyn. The sooner I can get a lawyer the sooner we can have you out of here. Keep your chin up, okay? And I'll be back as soon as I can.'

'Okay.' Lyn looked at him lovingly and tried hard to be brave. 'I guess I won't be going anywhere,' she managed.

He grinned. 'That's my girl!' His hands suddenly gripped her tightly and he pulled her roughly against him and kissed her hard on the mouth. 'You *are* my girl, Lyn,' he said forcefully, 'and I'm not going to let anything happen to you.'

Then he quickly let her go and strode purposefully out of the room, leaving Lyn standing alone until they came to take her away and lock her in a cell.

They brought her some food, but she couldn't eat, just walked up and down the little cell impatiently until Beric came back a couple of hours later with a solicitor. He questioned her about what had happened, but she could add nothing to what she had told the police. To her eager question he had, reluctantly, to tell her that on a serious charge like this there was no hope of the police letting her go straightaway, they would have to wait until the magistrates' court tomorrow. Lyn gripped Beric's hand tightly, but she merely nodded, willing herself not to get upset again. Beric had explained to the solicitor about his fingerprints theory and now he asked her if she had any idea who might have planted the dope on her.

Lyn shook her head. 'No, none. I certainly didn't see anyone do it.'

The solicitor looked at her over his glasses, his eyes not unsympathetic. 'You're in a state of shock at the moment, Miss Maxwell, which is perfectly understandable. But I want you to try and think very carefully back over your last flight and see if you can remember if and when anyone ever had the opportunity to do it. Will you do that?' He stood up.

'Yes. Yes, of course.' Lyn, too, stood up and shook the hand he held out to her. 'Thank you for coming so promptly.'

'Not at all.' He turned to say something to Beric, but just then the door opened and the detective-sergeant came in.

He looked round at the three of them grimly, then said, his voice harsh and sardonic, 'I have to tell you that we've had the results of the fingerprint tests. Miss Maxwell's prints exactly match some of those on the carton containing the heroin. There can be no doubt that she handled it before the Customs check.'

For a moment Lyn could only stare at him blankly, hardly taking it in. She was aware of Beric's face, suddenly white and drawn, turning to stare at her, but then the room started to sway and she fell to the floor in a dead faint.

That night was the worst that Lyn had ever known. She lay on the narrow bed and stared up at the dim light set into the ceiling, a light that was never switched off because someone came and checked on you once an hour; making sure she hadn't tried to hang herself, she supposed bitterly. She tried to do as the solicitor had asked her and think back over the flight, but her thoughts kept coming back to the nightmare of the present, and then she would turn her face into the hard pillow and weep silently, afraid that they might hear her.

In the morning her father came, rather flustered by

it all and inclined to be bombastic, demanding in his
ex-army officer's voice to know what was going on and
threatening the sergeant with dire consequences if he
didn't realise his mistake and let his daughter go at
once. He got short shrift from the police, who were
used to his kind of attitude, and had to go away and
wait at the court with Beric and the solicitor.

Lyn had been terrified of the ordeal, but when her
case came up it was all over in just a few minutes. She
only had to answer a few questions, then her solicitor
asked for bail and, as it was her first offence, the
magistrates granted it. Then she was free to go, to have
Beric's arm to hold on to and to walk out of the court
into the sunlight again.

But nothing was the same any more; Air International had immediately suspended her from duty, so
there was no job to keep her mind off her worries,
then the papers picked up the story and her mother
got terribly upset and said that if only she'd taken a
teacher training course as they'd wanted her to this
would never have happened. She said a lot of other
things too, and became so hysterical that they had to
send for the doctor. In the end it got so bad that her
father said Lyn had better go and stay with his Aunt
Mary, her great-aunt. But Aunt Mary lived way up in
Yorkshire, which meant that Lyn had to travel down
to London whenever she wanted to see her solicitor
and Beric. And Beric she wanted to see all the time,
she needed him badly, but he had his job to do. He
tried to transfer to European routes so that he could be
in England most of the time, but the airline proved
adamant and made him stay on the transatlantic run,
making it clear at the same time that they didn't like
his involvement with Lyn. But he ignored them and

did everything he could to help her, demanding that the police fingerprint everyone who had been on the plane. But this they refused to do; as far as they were concerned Lyn had been caught redhanded and the case was closed. It was like beating his head against a stone wall; there was just nothing he could do, except stand beside her and give her his moral support.

Her case came up for trial quite quickly and Lyn made another trip to London to meet the barrister that her solicitor had instructed to act for her. He went into everything all over again, questioning her very closely.

'Now, we'll take it from when you left Miami,' he told her. 'You took your bag on to the plane; where did you put it then?'

'In the central galley where all the cabin staff leave their bags.'

'So any of the cabin crew could have put the dope in it during the flight?'

'Yes, I suppose so,' Lyn agreed wretchedly. 'But why should they? If they'd known it was dangerous to have the drug during the flight then they would have known in Miami and not brought it with them. It doesn't make sense. It was only here in London that we realised anything was wrong.'

'All right, try and remember what happened when you landed. Did all the crew leave the plane together?'

'Yes,' Lyn nodded. 'We walked across the tarmac in a group.'

'Who were you with?'

'I was with Beric—Mr Dane.'

'No one else?'

'I came down the steps with a couple of girls, but Beric was waiting for me and I walked along with him.'

'And you had your bag with you the whole time?'

'Yes.'

'Were you carrying anything else?'

'Yes, my panda. A big toy panda bear I'd brought back from Miami.'

'So you were carrying two things. Was your bag open? It had a shoulder strap, didn't it? Could it have twisted round behind you while you were carrying your toy?'

Frowning to remember, Lyn said slowly, 'No, I don't think so. But it was open while I . . .' She stopped suddenly, her mind frozen, almost afraid to think of the memory that had suddenly come into her mind.

'You've thought of something?' the barrister said quickly. 'What is it?'

She didn't answer him immediately, but slowly she let the pictures come back. She had been groping in her bag for her passport but finding it difficult while she was carrying the panda, then Beric had taken the bag from her, had dropped behind for a few seconds while he looked for the passport and she had walked on, her back to him, then he had caught up to her, given her her passport and put the bag back on her shoulder.

It was Beric who had planted the dope on her! No one else had had the opportunity. It had to be him!

CHAPTER TWO

IMMEDIATELY the idea was rejected. Lyn shook her head decisively. 'No. No, it was nothing.'

But her face had gone very pale and the barrister looked at her shrewdly. 'Are you sure, Miss Maxwell? You must remember that this is a very serious charge and the authorities are clamping down especially hard on drug trafficking at the moment. It may very well be that, if you are convicted, you will be sent to prison,' he told her bluntly. 'So if there is even the slightest thing that you think might help your case you must tell me at once. Do you understand?' he added after a moment when she didn't speak, just sat staring down at the table between them.

Slowly Lyn nodded, her voice little more than a whisper as she answered, 'Yes, I—I understand.'

'And there is nothing you wish to tell me?' he probed.

Lyn's head came up and she said steadily, 'No, nothing.'

'I see.' He went on to tell her what to expect during the trial,' but Lyn hardly heard him, her thoughts elsewhere, her mind already beginning to be torn apart by doubts and uncertainties.

After the interview she went straight back to her hotel room and sat down on the bed, gazing unseeingly at the cream-painted walls. Her first instinct had been to reject any suggestion that Beric might have planted the dope on her. To accept the idea meant that she also had to accept that he really cared nothing for her, that he might even have been putting on an act just so that he could use her in this way if the necessity ever arose. Almost since they had first met, he had waited for her at the end of a flight and walked through Customs with her. It had always given her a big thrill, made her feel really great that he should single her out in this way in front of the rest of the crew. For a few moments her mind strayed, remembering the wonder and pride she had felt, but then she wrenched it determinedly back. She *had* to concentrate, had to.

Putting her balled fists up to her temples, Lyn tried to go through exactly what had happened after they had landed. Had anyone else had a chance to touch her bag? But there was no one, only Beric. She sighed wretchedly, searching desperately for some means of proving to herself that it couldn't have been him. Suddenly she sat up straight, her eyes brightening; if Beric had placed the talcum carton in her bag just before the Customs check then there wouldn't have been time for her prints to get on it. Her eyes glowed with excitement and relief. Of course! That was it. He couldn't possibly have done it. She hadn't touched her bag at all after that. Except—except—she bit her lip fiercely, her eyes bleak again—except after they had gone through passport control and she had slipped her passport back into her bag as she walked towards the Customs desk. Vividly now, she remembered that she'd had difficulty getting the hard-backed passport into her bag, had moved something else out of the way to make room for it, something round, cylindrical. The last vestige of colour drained from her face and she put her head in her hands and wept.

But even though her reason told her that it must

have been Beric, her emotions fought against accepting
it. She was so crazily in love with him that she just
couldn't believe that he could deliberately have done it
to her, and even less could she believe that he felt
nothing for her, that it had all been a big act to win her
over. She sat in the lonely hotel room for several hours
before she could bring herself to accept that there was
only one way to find out the truth; she would have to see
Beric and face him with it, find out one way or the other.

At present Beric was in Miami on a two-day stopover
and wouldn't be back until the day after tomorrow.
For a few moments she contemplated calling him there,
but then rejected the idea; she wanted to be able to see
his face when she asked him, to be able to read his
reaction.

The next two days were among the longest and the
loneliest in Lyn's life. She wandered aimlessly round
London, looking in shop windows or gazing unseeingly
at exhibits in museums and picture galleries. She didn't
eat much, her eyes had lost their old sparkle and her
face looked thin and drawn. At last the time arrived
for Beric to fly back and she went to meet him at the
airport. His flight was delayed and the extra hour she
had to wait, pacing restlessly up and down the reception area, was agonising. Then she saw him walking
briskly down the long corridor, taller than everyone
else, and looking round eagerly until he saw her, his
face breaking into a warm smile of greeting. Her heart
lurched and stood still, and for a few wonderful
seconds she felt as she had before, before her world
had been turned upside down by some stranger's greed
and evil. A stranger's—or Beric's? Her face had lit up
and she had instinctively moved to run towards him, but
now she stopped and waited, her face white and tense.

A quick look of concern wiped the smile from Beric's face and he walked rapidly up to her. 'Lyn, what is it?' He caught her arm and looked at her searchingly.

'I—I . . .' She found that she couldn't look at him and lowered her head. 'I have to talk to you. But not here.'

'All right. Let's go back to my place.'

'No, I'd rather go back to my hotel. Please.'

'Right.'

Still holding her arm, he led her out to the nearby car park reserved for flight crews and slung his bag in the trunk of his Italian sports car. It occurred to Lyn to wonder whether he had been searched this trip, and then she felt sick for even thinking it.

They were both silent in the car, Lyn because she was too wound up about what lay ahead to make small talk, and Beric because he was worried and didn't want to upset her, if the frequent, anxious looks he gave her were anything to go by.

Once inside her hotel room, Lyn walked nervously over to the window and stood staring out, trying to work up her courage to face him with it. After what seemed like an age she turned round and found him watching her speculatively.

'Beric, there's—there's something I have to ask you,' she managed, her nails digging into the palms of her hands as she balled them into tight fists at her side.

'There's something I have to ask you too,' Beric put in, his face stern.

Lyn blinked at him in surprise, completely taken aback. 'There—there is?'

'Yes.' He crossed the room to stand in front of her and put his hands on her shoulders. He had taken off his uniform cap and a lock of dark hair had fallen forward on to his forehead. His eyes, blue as an Aegean sky, smiled down at her. 'Did you miss me?' he demanded.

'Why—yes, of course I did.'

'Then how about welcoming me home?' he asked softly.

His hands slid down her back and drew her gently towards him. Lyn stared up into his eyes as if she was hypnotised. She wanted to resist, knew she ought to, but his head was coming down and then his lips were on hers, soft, insinuating, willing her to respond. For a moment she let herself savour the feel of his mouth, the initial softness that she knew would change and grow hard as his passion increased, the delicate, teasing kisses that stirred and excited her. He took her mouth, did what he wanted to it, while she stood in his arms, eyes closed, inert, neither resisting nor submitting.

But suddenly something seemed to snap inside her, her arms went up round his neck and she pressed herself fiercely against him, her mouth opening as she returned his kiss hungrily, passionately. For a moment Beric was startled and went to raise his head, but Lyn wound her fingers in his hair and pulled him down to her again, her lips urgent with desire, seeking the fulfilment that only he could give. Since that last trip to Miami, Beric's kisses had been reassuring, encouraging, his emotions held in check, but now he too, taken by surprise, gave way to passion, pulling her close against him, his hands caressing, his lips savage in their need.

For long minutes they clung together, Beric's mouth leaving hers to explore her throat, kiss her eyes, bite at the lobe of her ear, then he stooped down to pick her up and carry her to the bed. He laid her gently down on it and Lyn looked up at him as he bent over her, his breathing ragged. Thickly he said, 'That was one fantastic welcome—and then some!' He smiled at her. 'I think you do it on purpose.'

'What?'

'Try to drive me out of my mind. We were going to wait, remember?' He put his hand on her shoulder and gently began to massage it.

'Wait till when?' Lyn's eyes shadowed, became dark. 'Until I come out of prison, do you mean?' she said bitterly.

A muscle jerked in Beric's jaw and his hand tightened on her shoulder. 'You're not going to prison. Don't talk like that,' he ordered roughly.

Lyn gazed up at him, her face tense. 'Do you love me, Beric?'

His face softened and his mouth twisted in a rueful curve of amusement. 'I've an idea that's supposed to be my line.' Then his face grew serious again and he looked at her steadily. 'But the answer's yes, Lyn. I love you very much.'

Her lashes flickered for a second, but then she went on, 'Enough to go to prison for me, if you could?'

'Nobody's going to prison,' he answered roughly.

'But if you could?' she persisted.

Pain seemed to fill his eyes for a moment, then he said fiercely, 'Yes, I'd do anything to keep you from that.'

Lyn looked up at him, her face pale and set. 'In that case why did you put the dope in my bag, knowing that I'd be arrested?' she demanded icily.

He stared at her, as if he hadn't heard right, then his face slowly changed, became incredulous. He shook his head in bafflement. '*What* did you say?'

'You heard me clearly enough.'

'Yes, I did. But I just couldn't believe it.' He straightened up and looked at her in amazement. 'What is this, Lyn? What are you trying to say?'

Tiredly almost, she answered, 'I remembered, Beric. There's no point in denying it.'

'Denying *what*?' There was a harsh note now behind his bafflement.

Lyn pulled herself up into a sitting position and faced him, her eyes never leaving his. Clearly she said, 'I remembered that on that last flight we walked along together from the plane. I was carrying the panda and I couldn't find my passport in my bag. You took the bag from me and dropped behind for a few moments so that I couldn't see you. Then you caught up to me and gave me back the bag and my passport.' Her voice not much higher than a whisper but sounding very loud in the suddenly still room, she added, 'You were the only one, Beric. The only one other than me to touch my bag after we got off the plane.'

Beric's jaw tightened, then he was reaching for her hands and talking swiftly, urgently. 'Yes, I did take your bag from you—I remember doing it now. But you surely don't believe that *I* planted the dope on you? Lyn, you *can't* believe that I'd do a thing like that to you!' His grip tightened and his blue eyes gazed earnestly into hers. 'I've just told you that I love you. I've never said that to any other girl, Lyn—never! Do you really think that, feeling as I do, I'd let you worry or suffer for a second if I could avoid it—and especially be the cause of it? Do you?' he added forcefully, his tone imperative.

Lyn stared at him, wanting to believe him, wanting

desperately to trust him, but the cold voice of reason
in her brain yelled at her not to. Stubbornly she said,
'There was no one else; it had to be you.' Putting her
hands up to her temples, she shook her head in
agonised bewilderment and went on, 'I just want to
know whether you intended to do it all along, that's
all. Whether everything you said you felt for me was
just a lie, a pretence . . .'

'Stop it!' Beric had got to his feet and was bending
over her, his face white. He caught hold of her wrists
and pulled her hands down, hauling her to her feet.
'Lyn, I've told you—it wasn't me! I swear to you it
wasn't!'

Lyn gazed up into his taut face and her eyes closed
in pain. She mustn't look at him, mustn't listen to the
crying of her heart. Pulling her hands free, she said
dully, 'I don't believe you.'

Beric's face went white and his lips compressed into
a thin line. 'Do you have so little trust in me, then?' he
demanded harshly. 'You must care for me very little if
you think that I could do that to you!'

Feeling suddenly cold, Lyn crossed her arms over
her chest and held them tightly. Haltingly she said,
'That's where you're wrong. I love you so much that
I'd do almost anything for you, forgive anything. If
you'd come right out and said that you were desperate,
that you'd put the dope in my bag in a moment of
blind fear and panic, then I'd have stood by you. I
might have lost a lot of respect, but I'd have gone on
loving you. But to do it and then pretend you know
nothing about it, to even say that you were trying to
find the real culprit . . .' she shook her head helplessly,
'that I can't forgive or forget.'

A bleak look had come into Beric's eyes, but he said

determinedly, 'I've told you the truth, Lyn. And there's an easy way to prove it. If I had put the heroin in your bag then my fingerprints would be on the carton. We'll go down to the police station right now and ask them to take my prints and compare them with those they found.'

Again Lyn shook her head. 'Do you think I haven't already thought of that? But it wouldn't make any difference; no one but a fool would have left his own prints on the carton. You could easily have picked it up with a handkerchief or something.'

'I see,' he answered heavily. 'So nothing I can say will convince you that I'm telling the truth?'

'No.' Lyn looked at him and was filled with a sudden fierce anger. 'Oh, why the hell don't you tell the *real* truth? You know you did it, so why not admit it?' she yelled at him. 'Why go on pretending . . .'

Answering anger flared in Beric's face. He grabbed her arm and spun her round to face him. 'Pretending?' he repeated grimly. 'I'm beginning to wonder if you aren't doing some pretending of your own!'

'And just what's that supposed to mean?' Lyn demanded, glaring at him.

'You said that you were positive that no one else touched your bag. Well, I *know* I didn't put the heroin there. So that only leaves you, doesn't it?'

Lyn's face went chalk-white. 'What do you mean?'

'I mean that all these accusations you've suddenly decided to hurl at me could just be a cover-up for something you did yourself. Maybe I was wrong about you all along. Maybe that innocent, untouched look of yours was just an act to fool me and everyone else. You only had to smile at a Customs man and he'd wave you through. I don't remember your baggage

ever being checked before they got that last tip-off.'
His tone became contemptuous, almost a snarl. 'What
did you do it for, Lyn? Was it for the money, or was it
for yourself? Is that what it is? Are you a drug addict?'
Without warning, he jerked her arm and pulled her
against him, then, with his free hand, began to pull off
her jacket. 'Let's have a closer look at your arms, see
whether you have any needle marks.'

'Stop it! Leave me alone!'

Lyn began to struggle, beating against his chest with
her fists, but he easily dragged off her jacket and began
to push the sleeves of her shirt up her arms. Lyn came
up against the edge of the bed and fell on to it still
struggling. Beric knelt over her and held her while he
examined her arms. They were quite clean. He stood
up and said sardonically, 'So now we know you did it
for the money.'

'You filthy swine! You pig!' Lyn jumped to her feet
and hit him hard across the face. The slap cracked like
a whip and must have hurt him, but he hardly flinched.
His eyes had gone cold and steely, blue as long-frozen
ice.

'If you think I'm going to go to prison for you,
you're crazy!' she shouted furiously. 'You just used
me! The whole time you were just setting me up to use
me!' Her voice almost broke, but anger carried her on.
'But I'm not going to let you get away with it, do you
hear me? I might have been willing to take the blame
for you once, but not any more. Not now I've seen you
for what you really are.' She laughed, a harsh, stri-
dently mirthless sound. 'My God, I was blind! How
you must have sneered at me behind my back—the
naïve dupe who was wax in your hands, who fell for
you the first time you smiled at her. How you must

have laughed!' She trembled violently and turned away, unable to even look at him any longer.

There was a heavy silence, then Beric, his voice acid and bitter, said, 'I take it that that means you're going to go to the police and accuse me of planting the dope on you?'

'Yes, it does,' Lyn retorted without turning round.

'I see.' There was another pause, then he went on, 'I don't know whether you're acting or not, Lyn, but it doesn't much matter any more. If you're not, then dear God, I pity you, because you've trampled to death something that was precious and sweet. And if you are——' he shrugged and spoke with angry revulsion, 'then, luckily for me, you're also a fool. When I saw you today, so near the trial and without there being any hope of you being found innocent, I was willing to lie and say that I'd put the stuff in your bag. I'd have perjured myself and I'd have gone to prison for you, if I had to. But you were too ready with your accusations, Lyn. You shot my Sydney Carton act down in flames before I'd even had a chance to tell you.'

Lyn turned sharply to stare at him, her eyes searching his face.

'Yes,' he nodded heavily, 'ironical, isn't it? You could have got what you were playing for without any effort if only you'd waited for a while. I'd happily have taken the blame for you and you'd have been free to go on deceiving and tricking people—perhaps even going on smuggling once this fuss had died down. I wouldn't put it past you, you've nerve enough for anything.'

Lyn had been listening without speaking, her face set into a frozen mask of contempt and hate, but now she said derisively, 'What a consummate liar you are! Even now, when I know you for what you are, you're still trying to lie your way out of it.' With sudden violence, she added fiercely, 'Get out of my sight! I never want to see you again until the day I have the pleasure of seeing you in court being sentenced for what you've done!'

A murderous look came into Beric's eyes, he took a hasty step towards her and for a second Lyn thought that he was going to strike her, but then he turned sharply on his heel and walked quickly out of the room, slamming the door behind him.

It was the next morning before Lyn went to the police, after a long, wakeful night in which she had cried a lot for lost love, lost happiness, lost naïvety. The detective-sergeant in charge of her case listened to her story in silence. She spoke slowly, haltingly, even now reluctant to implicate Beric, but knowing that there was no alternative.

When she'd done the sergeant asked her one or two questions and then said shortly, 'What you've told me isn't new to me, Miss Maxwell. Mr Dane came to see me yesterday afternoon and told me he had reason to think that you would be accusing him of having planted the heroin on you. He admitted that he had remembered touching your bag after you had recalled the incident to his memory. But he insisted on making a statement, swearing that he did *not* put the stuff in your bag, did not remember seeing it there and saw no one else put it there. He also insisted on having his fingerprints compared with those on the carton. This was duly done and no trace of his fingerprints were found.' The sergeant lifted his head and looked at her steadily. 'As far as the police are concerned Mr Dane is completely in the clear and we will not be bringing any charges against him.'

The trial lasted only two days. Her parents didn't come, but Aunt Mary travelled down with her and sat near the front of the court where Lyn could see her, a slight but indomitable figure in her lilac coat and feathered hat. Lyn looked nervously round the court, but all the other faces, except that of her barrister, were strange to her. Everyone looked at her as she took her place in the dock and she felt like a freak being exhibited at a fair. The prosecution called several witnesses, including the Customs people, a narcotics expert, the detective-sergeant, then it was the turn of the defence, and her barrister did his best with very little to go on. He had wanted to call character witnesses: her old headmistress, the local vicar, whom she'd known all her life, but when her mother heard of it she had gone into hysterics again, saying that they'd have to move, she'd never be able to hold her head up in church or at the bridge club again. So Lyn, unwilling to upset her mother even more, had refused to let the barrister go ahead. So instead he called some of the stewardesses in the crew, who were of little help, all uncomfortable at being there and carefully avoiding looking at her after the first swift glance when they had entered the court. They all denied seeing anyone put the carton in her bag, but also said that they hadn't seen Lyn put it in her bag or act at all suspiciously. Then he called Beric. Lyn's heart lurched when he came into the room and she quickly looked away, her hands shaking.

The barrister questioned him very closely, trying to make him slip up and implicate himself, but he answered all the questions clearly and steadily. Yes, he realised that he had not admitted touching the bag when Miss Maxwell was first arrested, but it had only been for a few seconds and he had forgotten the incident, as she had until quite recently. No, as he'd told the police, he had not put the heroin in her bag and hadn't seen it there. There were lots more similar questions phrased in different ways, but he consistently and calmly denied any guilt, although his face grew paler and his hands tightened into fists at his side. Eventually the barrister had to reluctantly let him go. Then there was only a representative of the airline who said that, although Lyn had only been with them a short time, she had always appeared to be honest and there had never been a hint of any earlier trouble, and the defence was all over except for her own evidence and cross-examination, which hardly took any time at all since all she could do was deny the accusation.

There was a break for lunch after her barrister had wound up the case for the defence, a break in which Lyn went with Aunt Mary to a nearby restaurant and just sat and stared at the plate of food in front of her. Her great-aunt didn't try to press her, just talked inconsequentially on about the doings in the little country village where she lived, but when, at one point, Lyn's hand began to tremble violently, Aunt Mary reached out and held it tightly in her own, trying to transmit some of her own undaunted courage that had seen her first love lost in the war, and later her husband and only child killed in a road accident.

Lyn gripped her hand and tried to smile through eyes heavy with unshed tears. 'Dear Aunt Mary,' she said huskily. 'What should I do without you?'

Her aunt smiled, but said earnestly, 'The strength is within yourself, my dear. No matter what happens to you when we go back in that courtroom, I know that you'll find the courage to face it with dignity and fortitude. And always remember that I believe in your innocence implicitly. I'll be there whenever you need me, helping in any way I can.' She flushed slightly and sat back, her manner becoming brisk. 'But that's enough of such serious talk.' Lifting up her hand, she called the waiter over. 'What you need now is a large brandy to get you through the afternoon.'

So it was with rather a light head that Lyn went back into court and listened to the judge's summing-up. It seemed that her barrister had been right in thinking that the authorities were clamping down on drug-trafficking, because the judge kept stressing the serious nature of the case and his summing-up was so against her that it was little short of bias. He pointed out that, although the defence had done their utmost to shift the blame on to someone else, there was absolutely no evidence to prove that this was so, whereas everything pointed to her own involvement. He again mentioned the seriousness of the charge and sent the jury out to consider their verdict. After such a summing-up it was no surprise to anyone when they returned within twenty minutes and gave a unanimous verdict of guilty.

The judge turned to look at Lyn and said, 'Lynette Maxwell, you have been found guilty of the serious charge of smuggling narcotics into this country. In view of your refusal to help the police in any way to trace the people who handed you the drugs or those to whom you were to pass it on, I have no choice but to send you to prison for a term of three years.'

Lyn stood as if turned to stone for a long moment, then she slowly turned her head and looked round the courtroom, trying to find Beric to let him see the hatred and contempt in her face. But he wasn't there, he hadn't stayed to hear the verdict. Then a policewoman put her hand on Lyn's arm and she turned and walked numbly from the court.

CHAPTER THREE

THREE years is a long time. A person's character can change radically in that period, especially when they are thrust into an environment that is wholly foreign to them and forced to accept a régime and companions which they would normally never have encountered.

For the first few weeks in the women's prison Lyn existed in a state of numb apathy, doing as she was told, working, sleeping, eating barely enough to keep her alive, taking little notice of her fellow inmates. Her father came to see her once, sitting uncomfortably and finding nothing very much to say, surreptitiously glancing at his watch all the time in the hope that he had been there long enough and could decently take his leave. Her mother, it seemed, had been unable to bear the thought of entering a prison; just the idea of it had made her feel ill. When he at last stood up to go, Lyn told him that she'd rather he didn't come again. He blustered a bit, but there was an overwhelming look of relief on his face as he finally agreed. He promised to write, and he did for a few months, then the letters tailed off until they arrived only on Christmas and birthdays. It didn't matter, Lyn knew that there would never be any chance of going back to live with them; whether they believed her to be innocent or not they wouldn't want her back there, an ever-present reminder of the stigma that had blighted their comfortable, well-ordered lives.

But Aunt Mary came, travelling down from Yorkshire regularly once a month, bringing with her a breath of all that was sane and good in the world, talking of the little things that had happened to her and quite unperturbed by the warders and having to talk across a table with lots of other prisoners and their visitors in the same room. Then one month she didn't come, and instead Lyn received a letter from her solicitor saying that Aunt Mary was very ill; she had an incurable disease that had been worsening for some time. She had been ordered by her doctors to take a complete bed rest, but had insisted on visiting Lyn, and the exhaustion caused by the travelling had exacerbated her condition. A week later she died.

Lyn asked the prison governor for permission to go to her funeral, but, because Aunt Mary wasn't a close enough relative, this was refused. It was then that Lyn's final apathy dropped away and the hate that was already festering inside her took over. This was intensified by the strong feelings of guilt she felt about Aunt Mary; if she hadn't come to visit Lyn she might still be alive. The information that Aunt Mary had left her everything she owned only made things worse. She felt like a murderess. She was probably the richest woman in Holloway, but all she felt was hatred, and the urgent need for revenge on the man who had put her there!

Soon it became an obsession, filling her every waking thought and many of her dreams and nightmares. *How* to get her revenge was the problem; she had many ideas, but although they would have given her a great deal of satisfaction, they were far from practical or even possible. The main thought that stayed in Lyn's mind, that continually kept her brain going round and round the problem, was an almost fanatical desire to see the table turned, to have Beric caught with some heroin on him and to see him put in prison as he deserved. But perhaps the narrowness of his escape might have scared him off and he was steering clear of the racket? Lyn thought not; with eyes newly opened to the failings of humanity, she thought that he might stop for quite a long time, but eventually greed would make him start to smuggle the stuff again. And she, or an agent working for her, had to be on hand to expose him when he did. Even if he didn't go back to it there could be ways to get what she wanted. Her mouth twisted in wry amusement; how ironical it would be if Beric was caught with dope that someone else had planted on *him*!

Feeding on hate, using it to keep from going under in that terrible place, Lyn gradually began to work towards attaining her goal. She didn't hurry, she had plenty of time to do it in, three whole years in which to plan and prepare.

Her first idea was to hire an agent to act for her, someone she could pay to get close to Beric, find out his movements so well that he could be either caught when bringing some dope into the country or else have some planted on him. It wasn't an idea that appealed to her all that much for two main reasons: (1) how far could she trust someone who was being paid, and who, if there was a chance that he might get caught, would bungle things or even implicate her; (2) although there would be the satisfaction of knowing that she had been revenged if it succeeded, it would only be at second hand. She wanted to see the look on Beric's face when the heroin was found on him, wanted to see him suffer. But most of all she wanted him to know that it was *she* who had set him up. Only that would give her the vengeance her soul craved. But there was no way she could get near Beric without him seeing her and guessing her intentions. He would be bound to see, the hate would be there in her eyes, naked and burning, there was no way she could pretend that she'd forgiven him, wanted to start over again, even if he'd let her. No, it had to be an agent.

With this end in view, Lyn began to look around her. It was comparatively easy to find out why the other women were in prison once she began to come out of her shell and mix and talk with the others, and to seek out and get to know those she thought might be suitable. Not that she had definitely decided on a woman, it might be that one of them might lead her to a man who would be able to do the job better. She also made very careful enquiries about getting hold of a quantity of heroin in case she should need it to plant on Beric. She went about the task methodically, gradually getting to know the tougher, hardened criminals or the girls who associated with underworld gangs outside, and because she didn't push or criticise she began to get the information she wanted. But who to get to act for her was still the big stumbling block, until she began talking to a very beautiful girl she thought might be a possibility. Her name was Nadia Claremont and she had achieved some fame as a newspaper model until she had been caught trying to sell a diamond bracelet that her boy-friend had stolen, while wearing a mink coat that came from another burglary.

She proved to be too dumb for Lyn's purpose, but she was a feast of information about the underworld of criminals in London, and Lyn talked to her quite a lot in the hope of making a useful contact. They became quite friendly, and one Sunday afternoon were sitting together in Nadia's cell when she pulled out some photographs to show Lyn. They were mostly posed pin-ups with very few clothes, that had appeared in the papers, and Lyn duly admired them. Then a smaller photograph fell to the floor and she bent to pick it up. It was of a mousey-haired young girl with a long nose and rather buck teeth. A pair of National Health glasses perched on her nose and she was dressed in a rather shapeless blouse stretched tight over her large bosom, a dark skirt and sensible shoes.

Lyn handed the photo back. 'Who's that? A relation of yours?' she asked without real interest.

Nadia laughed. 'You could say that. That was Maureen Higgins.'

'Was? Is she dead?'

Nadia laughed again, her voice full of merriment. 'Yes, I suppose she is.' She looked at the photo reminiscently, then turned to Lyn and said, 'That's me, love. Before I had the works.'

Lyn stared at her and then again at the snapshot. 'But it can't possibly be, it's nothing like you. You're beautiful, and that girl is plain.'

'Anybody can be beautiful if they had what I've had done to me.' Nadia leaned back against the wall and began to explain. 'I looked like that until I was about eighteen, then I met this old geezer who reckoned he could turn me into a film star. Well, of course, I just laughed. I mean—look at me! How could you make a Brigitte Bardot out of that? But he said yes, he could, and took me along to a cosmetic surgeon he knew. He used to have a place in Harley Street, but he fixed the faces of a few criminals on the side and got found out, so they struck him off, or whatever it is they do to doctors. Anyway, to cut a long story short, he altered my nose and did something to the shape of my eyes and chin, and then a dentist did the work on my teeth so they didn't stick out. I had a few weeks in a health farm to get rid of the fat, had my hair dyed blonde, contact lenses instead of glasses, and here I am, Nadia Claremont instead of Maureen Higgins.'

'It's fantastic!' Lyn said incredulously. 'I'd never have believed it. No one would ever recognise you.'

Nadia went on to say something else, but Lyn wasn't listening. She was staring at the photograph and thinking hard, her eyes suddenly wide and bright. Abruptly she turned to the other girl. 'How much did it cost?' she demanded.

'A few thousand, I should think. Though mind you, I didn't pay, the old geezer paid for it all, although I had to repay him later, if you see what I mean. But then I met Benjy and he took me away from him.'

'Do you know if this cosmetic surgeon is still fixing faces?' Lyn enquired eagerly, uninterested in Nadia's love life.

'Yes, I think so.' The other girl looked at her. 'Why the interest?'

'Nadia, do you think he could change my face, make me look beautiful?'

'You're all right as you are—not with a face like the back of a bus like I had. What do you want to have your face altered for?'

'I want to look different,' Lyn said quickly. 'I want to start a new life completely when I get out of here.'

'Well, I can understand that,' Nadia agreed. 'But look,' she hesitated, 'this beauty bit—it's not all that it's cracked up to be. Oh, it was all very lovely at first, having your photo in the papers and men wanting to take you out and that. But after a while it starts to get you down. Men take you out expecting only one thing in return, your boy-friends get jealous if you look at another man, and women aren't friendly any more because they don't like the opposition. And if you do settle down with a man and trust him, he only does the dirty on you—gets you put inside this place,' she added bitterly, then shrugged. 'Maybe when I get out I'll save up and get the doctor to alter my face again.'

Lyn looked at her curiously. 'You'd go back to being Maureen Higgins?'

Nadia took the photograph from her and laughed, then raised her eyebrows. 'Well, perhaps not quite as far as that.' Then, serious again, she added, 'But if I had a face like yours I definitely wouldn't want to change it.'

'But I would,' Lyn told her firmly. 'Very much.'

Nadia looked at the determination in her eyes and then nodded. 'All right, it's your face. I'll let you know how to contact him when you get out.'

As the months dragged slowly by Lyn's plans began to take a clearer shape in her mind and she assiduously applied herself to making them as perfect as possible. To that end she attended all the language classes that were available in the prison as well as paying a Frenchwoman who was a fellow prisoner to give her lessons in conversation. In her schooldays she had always been good at languages, a talent which had helped her to get the job with Air International, and she hoped to be able to put the talent to good use in her pursuit of Beric.

During her sentence she was often interviewed by the prison social workers, who tried to draw her out and warn her away from associating with the more hardened criminals, but they found themselves trying to knock down a stone wall with feather dusters. Lyn would sit through the interview with a cold, set face and answer their questions with a polite yes or no, giving nothing of herself away. She realised that they had their jobs to do, but she intended to make quite sure that she had all the contacts she needed when she got out, even if it meant associating with the very worst elements in the prison. So they had to let her go, baffled and annoyed by her attitude, and it was because of this that she wasn't sent to an open prison to finish her sentence, instead having to stay in Holloway the whole time. But this suited Lyn well; she much preferred to stay in contact with the people she thought might prove useful.

The day before she was released the prison Governor gave her a lecture about never getting into trouble again because it would be far worse for her a second time. She also went on about having served her punishment and being able to start a new life, make a new beginning, which made Lyn laugh inwardly; she was going to start a new life all right! This made her thoughts go to her plans for getting her own back on Beric and she dwelt on them lovingly, savouring every detail, and she didn't realise that the Governor had finished speaking until the silence penetrated her thoughts.

Slowly her eyes became aware of her surroundings and she looked at the Governor, who sighed and said tartly, 'I can see you've taken in absolutely nothing of what I've been saying. Well, I have no choice but to set you free tomorrow morning, much as I think you ought to stay inside. From your stubborn attitude to authority ever since you came here, it's quite obvious that you intend to do something that will have you back here before too long. But I can only warn you

that you will do yourself a great deal of harm by it.'
She paused, waiting for Lyn to speak, but when she
only continued to stand, stony-faced, the Governor
nodded and said sharply, 'Very well, Maxwell, you
may go.'

Lyn hadn't told her parents that she was coming out
and had no expectation of being met, so she was surprised and touched when she stepped outside the
prison gates at eight o'clock on the chilly, grey
November morning to see Nadia Claremont waiting
for her in a taxi.

'Hi. Welcome back to so-called civilisation,' Nadia
greeted her, a smile on her face as Lyn got into the
taxi. 'Here, you may as well start as you mean to go
on.' She held out a crystal tumbler filled with a liquid
that bubbled and sparkled in the glass.

Lyn looked at it and then at Nadia. 'Not champagne?' she said incredulously.

'The very same. Cheers.' Nadia raised her glass in
salutation and took a long drink. 'Mmm, nice.'

Sipping at hers, Lyn savoured the taste of it on her
tongue, felt the bubbles breaking on her nose. She
laughed and turned to Nadia, suddenly felt tears
pricking at the back of her eyelids. 'Thanks, Nadia,'
she said huskily. 'I didn't . . . I didn't expect . . .' She
looked away hastily.

'It's all right, love, I know.' Nadia's hand came out
to cover hers for a moment, then she laughed and said,
'Come on, drink up. I'll give you a toast. To hell with
all men!'

Lyn raised her glass. 'Oh, yes, I'll *definitely* drink to
that!' she agreed forcefully.

They went back to Nadia's flat where Nadia cooked
breakfast while Lyn lay and soaked in a hot bath

brimming with softly scented bubbles.

After they had eaten Nadia sat back and lit a cigarette. 'How do you want to spend your first day out?' she enquired. 'Go shopping for some new clothes? Or just sit around by yourself and listen to the silence? I know that's what I did, although I'd made loads of other plans before I got out, but I found it difficult to adjust for a while. If you do, I'll clear out and leave you alone.'

Lyn shook her head. 'Thanks, Nadia, but no. I want to fix up to have my face done. Did you contact the surgeon for me?'

'Do you still want to go ahead with that? You might change your mind after you've been outside for a few weeks.'

'No, I won't change my mind,' Lyn told her shortly. 'Did you see him?'

Nadia nodded. 'Yes. He can do it for you whenever you're ready, but you'll have to pay half of the money in advance.'

'That's okay. I need two days to take care of a couple of things and then I'll have it done. Where do I have to go?'

'He has a private nursing home in Sussex. I'll phone up and tell him you'll be there next week, then?'

'Yes. And once I've had my face done I shall need a new passport and a driver's licence.'

'What's wrong with your old ones?' Nadia objected. 'You could just have a new photograph put in the passport.'

'No, because I intend to change my name as well.'

'Use an alias, you mean?'

'Yes, that's right. And I shall need someone who can make some enquiries for me. A private detective or

someone like that—a person who can keep his mouth
shut. Do you know a man like that?'

'Yes, I can get you someone.' Nadia shook her head
at her. 'But I hope you know what you're doing, Lyn.'

'Oh, I know, all right,' Lyn assured her. 'I know
exactly what I'm doing.'

Having spent the night in Nadia's flat, the next
morning Lyn travelled by train to her parents' home.
As she walked up the drive of the large mock-Tudor
house she saw her father in the garden, cutting off the
heads of the dead roses. Lyn paused a moment by a
small tree and watched him. He seemed very content
as he worked, smoking a pipe and humming a tune to
himself. Slowly she walked forward and he looked up.

'Good morning, can I . . .' He broke off and stared,
a mixture of emotions in his face. 'Lyn!' Then he
smiled and held out a hand. 'My dear child!'

A surge of need and longing filled her and for a
moment she was on the verge of running to him and
hugging him, but then she remembered the long,
empty years and the impulse died. Calmly she said,
'Hallo, Father. How are you?'

The smile faded from his face and he lowered his
hand, looking embarrassed. He greeted her and took
her inside through the french windows into the sitting-
room where her mother was sitting at an antique desk,
writing a letter.

'Look who's here, Elizabeth,' her father said over-
heartily.

Her mother turned round with a smile that froze
into shocked horror chased by disbelief, anger and fear.
Lyn watched the play of emotions on her face with
fascination, realising that her mother had cut her out
of her life, put her so far out of her mind that she

might just as well have died. Obviously it had never occurred to either of them that the three years was up and she would be coming home. Home—Lyn laughed derisively to herself—she would never be able to call this place home again; Beric had taken that away from her as well as three years of her life.

They did their best under the circumstances, bringing coffee and cakes and trying to make stilted conversation but afraid of saying the wrong thing. Uncomfortable and on edge, wondering how to tell her that they didn't want her living with them any more. Lyn let them suffer for a while, feeling bloody-minded, but then had a revulsion of feeling as a wave almost of pity engulfed her. Poor things, it wasn't their fault their lives had been upset in this way. If they'd managed to put it behind them and forget, or at least pretend it had never happened, that their spoiled only daughter had ceased to exist on the day she had been found guilty, then good for them. Who was she to disrupt it all?

Bluntly Lyn told them that she had decided to live abroad in future—where, she wasn't quite sure, but she would let them know when she had a permanent address. The relief on their faces was magical, even though they tried to hide it. She left soon after, knowing that she would never go there again, and didn't once look back as she walked briskly down the drive.

The next day found her again on a train, going to York this time to see Great-Aunt Mary's solicitors. There she signed several papers and took possession of her aunt's jewellery, mostly older-style pieces that Aunt Mary herself had inherited. The house itself and most of the furniture had already been sold, Lyn having instructed them to keep back just a few antique

pieces that her aunt had been especially fond of and
which Lyn now left in their present storage. Heaven
alone knew when she would have a place of her own in
which to put them. For a moment she felt slightly
wistful, but she quickly pushed the feeling away; that
wasn't important. All that mattered now was making
Beric pay for the wrong that had been done her. She
hurried to catch the train to London, all the business
taken care of, her one thought now on her plans for
revenge.

Six weeks later Lyn again went to Nadia's flat. She
rang the bell and waited until her friend opened the
door.

'Yes?' Nadia looked at her enquiringly, no trace of
recognition in her blue eyes.

'Miss Claremont? I'm a follow-up social worker
attached to the prison service. I'm calling to . . .'

'Oh, are you?' Nadia began belligerently. 'Well, you
can just clear off! If you think I want anything to do
with . . .' She stopped suddenly as Lyn leaned against
the doorway and began to laugh. 'Just who are you?'
she demanded suspiciously.

'Oh, Nadia, it's me—Lyn. I'm sorry to tease you,
but I just had to assure myself that even someone who
knew me quite well wouldn't recognise me.'

'Good God! Even your own mother wouldn't recognise you. Come on in.' Nadia stood back to let Lyn
walk past and stood staring at her, shaking her head in
wonder. 'If I didn't know I'd never believe it. It's not
only your nose he's done. There's something else.'

Lyn nodded. 'He shortened my chin a little and
pulled back the skin at my temples to make my eyes
look wider apart. Then I went to a beautician who

plucked my eyebrows into a much finer line and dyed my hair blonde. And of course wearing it drawn straight back off my head when I always had a fringe before helps a lot.'

'But your eyes are a different colour—you had lovely brown eyes before. And your lashes look different too.'

'Mm, I had the lashes bleached blonde and I use grey-coloured lenses for my eyes.'

'Wow!' Nadia stood back and studied her. 'Well, you got your money's worth, Lyn. With those elegant new clothes and that hairstyle—there's no doubt about it, you really are beautiful. Beautiful and sophisticated.'

Turning to look in the long mirror fixed to the wall, Lyn said anxiously, 'Do you *really* think that, Nadia? You're not just saying it to please me? It's so important, you see.'

'No, I'm not just saying it. You're beautiful. Ice-cold—but beautiful.'

Lyn stared at herself in the glass. 'I still can't believe it's me,' she admitted. 'I see my reflection in a shop window and feel envious of the girl walking by, then I realise who it is and just stand and stare. People must think I'm mad.'

Nadia led her into the sitting-room and poured her out a drink. 'Here's to the new you. What's your new name going to be?'

'I thought about that a lot, and I've decided to keep my christian name as near to the old one as I can so that I'll remember to answer to it. So I thought Netta for the christian name as my name is Lynette.' And also, she thought to herself, because Beric only ever knew her as Lyn, which he probably thought was short for Linda, a common mistake that people had always made with her name, and she was quite sure that she'd never told him it was Lynette.

'And your surname?'

'Oh, anything will do for that. Give me some ideas.' Nadia looked thoughtful. 'You really want something simple. How about Page or Morgan or something like that?' She picked up a newspaper and glanced through it. 'Perhaps there's something in here. Yes, how does Lewis grab you?'

'Netta Lewis.' Lyn tried it a couple of times. 'Yes, I think I like it. It goes together. Right, that's settled, then. From now on I'm Netta Lewis.'

'So I suppose you'll want the fake passport done now?'

'Yes, please. I've brought the money with me. And I've had some photographs taken.' She fished them out of her bag and handed them to Nadia. 'How long will it take?'

'About a week, I should think. Is that all right?'

Lyn nodded. 'Yes, that's fine.'

They talked for a while longer and arranged to meet for a shopping expedition in a couple of days. Nadia asked her to stay, but it suited Lyn to book into a hotel. Her next visit was to a large department store where she bought a wig as much like her old colour and style of hair as possible, then, wearing this and without the grey contact lenses, she went to see the detective she had hired before she went into the clinic. The fewer people who knew about her change of appearance the better.

He was good at his job and well worth the five hundred pounds she had paid him to find out everything there was to know about Beric. His report contained a great deal of extra details but boiled down to the vital facts that Beric was still flying with Air International, was now a Captain and was on the London–Singapore route. He was still single, not engaged, and didn't seem to have a serious relationship with anyone, although he had, during the six weeks of the surveillance, spent a night with two different women. The report also gave his London address, which was the same as when Lyn had known him, the name of the hotel in Singapore where the air crews stayed on layovers, and details of future flight schedules for the next two months. Lyn raised her eyebrows when she saw those; such information was usually only available to a few vetted executives.

She listened, asked a few questions, and then sat back in her chair, satisfied. She had everything she needed now to put her plans into operation.

Two weeks later, secure in her new identity, she flew to Singapore.

The hotel where the Air International crews stayed was in the three-star grade and quite close to the airport, and Lyn had no difficulty in booking a modest single room with shower on the eleventh floor. From the schedule that the detective had obtained for her, she knew that Beric and his crew weren't due to arrive there for another ten days, having just left, so she immediately set about finding herself a job. She visited several employment bureaux and telephoned one or two places that she saw in the local paper. She went to six interviews, none of which were entirely suitable for her purposes. Then she struck lucky; she was offered a post as a teacher in a school run for English-speaking children, mostly the offspring of British and American businessmen whose companies had branches in Singapore. She was to teach French four mornings a week and double as a spare teacher whenever any of the other staff were ill or away for any reason. This would give her a reason for being in Singapore and also plenty of free time, but the beauty of it was that the school wasn't too far from the hotel, which gave her the perfect excuse for staying there.

Much to her surprise she had been offered every job for which she was interviewed. She had expected getting a job in a foreign country to be the hardest part of her plans and had been prepared for a long wait before the right one came along. What she hadn't taken into account was the effect of her appearance. The moment she walked into an office, tall, cool and sophisticated, every boss had perked up, realising that she would be an asset to any firm, and probably hoping to score with her themselves.

It took Lyn a while to realise that men's attitudes towards her had changed with her face. Before she met Beric she had had several boy-friends, some of whom had become quite passionate on occasion, usually after a few drinks and in the back seat of their cars down a dark lane, when Lyn had fought them off quite happily, knowing it was all part of the game. And none of them had got really serious, they hadn't sent her flowers or poems, hadn't looked for her as she entered a room, their faces lighting up. Even Beric, who had said he loved her, hadn't treated her like a fragile object, as something precious to be adored. Lyn's eyes grew bleak; but then that was hardly surprising, because he hadn't really been in love with her at all. But now when men looked at her they did so lingeringly, admiration in their eyes, often turning to watch her as she walked by. And they tried to chat her up far more, too. It had started back in England at the travel agent's where she had booked her ticket, and continued with the man who had sat next to her on the plane on the way over. Even in Singapore, where there were relatively few Europeans, several men had tried to approach her.

At first Lyn had been embarrassed, unsure of herself after being shut away from men for so long, and not knowing how to squash them, but she soon learnt that to be ice-cold and reserved usually worked; few of them had the nerve to go on after such a deliberate brush-off. And the fact that her beauty was man-made instead of natural helped her to keep a level head and see the advances for what they were worth.

Lyn had been working at the English school for three days when Beric's flight was due in. As the day came nearer tension built up inside her, although she had no intention of even showing herself to him; her plan called for far more subtlety than that. All she wanted to do while he was here on this lay-over was to get to know the stewardesses in his crew by sight and let them see her several times, and perhaps, if she could contrive it, exchange a smile with some of them. All she wanted to do was to establish herself as a resident of the hotel, so that when they came again they would recognise her and perhaps speak to her of their own accord. That way, it would appear that they had got to know her instead of the other way around.

On the day they were due to arrive, Lyn lingered in the crowded streets on the way back from the school, a tight ball of tension in her chest, afraid now to embark on the revenge she had nurtured for so long. What if she couldn't go through with it? What if just seeing Beric again made her go crazy and she let him know who she was, let him see and feel the hatred? But the knowledge that she had to be there when they checked in, had to see the stewardesses in their uniforms so that she would recognise them in everyday clothes, made her at last turn in the direction of the hotel.

She had cut it fine; an airport bus was just pulling into the forecourt as she went up the steps. It took all the will-power she possessed not to run across the foyer to the lifts, not to look back to see if it was him. But she managed somehow to walk unhurriedly to the desk and calmly ask the receptionist for her key. The Malayan youth smiled and handed it to her, knowing her number off by heart by now.

'There is also a letter for you, Miss Lewis.'

Lyn took it in surprise, then smiled as she recognised Nadia's rather childish handwriting. Her former fellow prisoner had turned out to be the best friend Lyn had ever had, trying to persuade her not to do anything foolhardy, but when she couldn't, doing her best to help, even at some risk to herself. If Lyn's forged passport was ever discovered and the police learnt where she had got it, they would both be back inside.

The surprise of the letter had distracted her for a few seconds, but now Lyn froze as a deep, authoritative, and all too well remembered voice spoke to the receptionist farther along the desk. Carefully not looking in that direction, Lyn turned with the letter in her hand and walked over to a central island surrounded by outward-facing cushioned seats. Choosing one facing the desk, Lyn sat down and opened the letter, pretending to give it all her attention while looking over it at the stewardesses in their smart navy blue uniforms. A different one from that which she had worn, Lyn noted; this one was far better designed and had a neat waistcoat under the fitted jacket.

She tried to keep her eyes fixed on the stewardesses, to make mental notes of their appearance, but even though she desperately willed herself not to, her eyes kept straying to Beric's broad back as he filled in a form at the desk. Then he half turned to speak to the First Officer and she saw his profile before she hastily looked down at her letter again, heart thumping crazily in her chest. But even in that one swift glance she had sensed that there was something different about him, but what it was she couldn't tell exactly. She would have to study him more closely to find out.

The crew members collected their keys, picked up their bags and walked over to the lifts. Lyn managed to get a grip on herself and study the six stewardesses as they passed, until she was sure that she would recognise them again. One of the male stewards caught sight of her as they waited and nudged his companion, who also turned to eye her appreciatively. Lyn looked down at the letter again; it wouldn't help her plans at all if one of the other men in the crew made a pass at her; it was only Beric she had designs on. By the time all the crew members had got into it the lift was full. Lyn sat and watched the numbers over the lift light up as it rose through the building. It stopped on the seventh and twelfth floors. Which probably meant that the cockpit crew were on the seventh and the lowly cabin staff on the twelfth, one floor above her own.

When they had gone, Lyn sat for some time just staring blindly, recovering from one of the most traumatic moments in her life. Almost she wished she *had* employed an agent rather than have gone through the last ten minutes, but she had got through it somehow, and without doing anything crazy, even though it would take quite some time before her heartbeat and pulse were even halfway back to normal. For the moment she couldn't really analyse her feelings; when she had heard his voice she had been hit by a great wave of emotions: hate, memories, pain, they had all welled up inside her so that for a while she hadn't even been able to think clearly.

On unsteady legs Lyn got up, the unread letter still clutched in her hand, and took the next lift up to her room. There she slowly sank down on to the bed and reaction set in as she began to tremble, her whole body shaking convulsively.

It was the next afternoon before she saw any of the crew again. After returning from the school she ate her lunch in the hotel restaurant and saw two of the girls also eating there. By hurrying through her own meal she was able to stand just behind them in the line at the cash desk on the way out and contrived to drop her bill so that she had to say 'Excuse me' to one of them.

The girl moved out of the way, smiled, and to Lyn's pleased surprise, said, 'Are you British?'

'Why, yes, I am.' Lyn returned the smile. 'How could you guess after only two words?'

The other girl laughed. 'Oh, we're used to guessing people's nationalities. We do it all the time. And an American would have said pardon me, not excuse me.'

It was Lyn's turn to pay then and she turned away as they walked off together towards the lifts, after giving her a friendly nod of farewell. They were still waiting for a lift when Lyn came out of the restaurant, and for a few seconds she hesitated, wondering whether to go up to them, but then she decided not to push it and went in the other direction, towards the foyer.

The next day Lyn managed to share a lift with one of the other girls and exchanged a nod and a smile with the first two, so she was well pleased with the success of her plan so far. In the evening she was sitting in an obscure corner of the foyer when she saw the whole crew, dressed in evening clothes, go out together. She was able to look at Beric for longer now, but still couldn't pinpoint what was different about him. He put his arm round one of the stewardesses in a casual gesture, smiling down at her, his lean face tanned and handsome. Something jerked in Lyn's heart as she remembered the way he used to look at her, and she wondered if he was having an affair with the stewardess. Then an icy chill gripped her as it occurred to her that he might just be setting up the other girl as he had her, ready to be used in case there was any danger of his being caught. The ball of hatred hardened and her eyes grew very cold and determined. The sooner she showed Beric up for what he was, the better.

On the following day the crew flew back to London and Lyn was able to relax and to formulate the details of her campaign for their next lay-over. She just hoped that the crew would consist of the same people and that the girls she had spoken to wouldn't be on a different flight. In the meantime she settled into her job and explored the teeming city a little, but she didn't go too far, preferring the delightful privacy of her own room and walks in the nearby park where she could just sit in the sun and watch the birds and revel in the feeling of freedom after being shut away for so long.

When the crew checked into the hotel for the second time Lyn sat with her back to them, watching through one of the huge mirrors that hung on the wall in the foyer. To her relief it was the same crew, and from their friendliness it looked as if they regularly flew together, which was fine as long as they didn't always go around in a crowd and would resist an outsider trying to join them. But everything went better than she had dared hope. On their very first evening she managed to bump into one of the girls she had spoken to in the restaurant queue and get into conversation with her while waiting to be served at the snack bar this time, and then it only seemed natural for them to sit together while they ate.

The girl's name was Julia Connors and she came from Norfolk. She seemed a very open and friendly girl and quite ready to talk about herself and the rest of the crew.

'How long have you been flying?' Lyn asked her casually, and then breathed a small sigh of relief when Julia answered, 'Two years.' Lyn hadn't recognised any of the stewardesses from the old days, but she wasn't very good at faces and it just made things that bit easier if the girl she used to get to Beric had never even heard of her.

Lyn told the other girl a little about herself, keeping as near to the truth as possible by saying that she'd been left a little money and had decided to travel, but didn't have enough to be completely independent and so had taken a part-time job while she was here. She didn't actually say it, but she let it be understood that she had also been teaching before she came out here.

'Do you always fly on this route?'

'If I can,' Julia told her. 'It's hard work and the jet lag can get pretty bad at times, but the crew are good fun and you can go to some interesting places from here.'

'The captain isn't too stern, then?' Lyn said laughingly, trying to make her tone as light as possible.

'Beric? Oh, no, he's not a bit like that. Deadly serious when he's flying, of course, but good fun on the ground when we all go out together. Not that he does that too often, he's usually with the men or with a girl.'

'One of the stewardesses?' Lyn asked, remembering the one he had put his arm round.

But Julia shook her head. 'No, that's one of his firm rules. He never goes out with any of us.' For a moment she looked wistful, then shrugged. 'Not that he's married or anything, but he's usually able to find plenty of women outside the airline.'

Lyn looked at Julia and raised her eyebrows. 'Oh, he's one of those, is he—a womaniser?'

Julia laughed. 'Wait till you see him, you'll understand why. He's thirty-three, tall, dark and handsome, and with the most gorgeous eyes. You might even fall for him yourself.'

Lyn laughed. 'Oh, I'm not in the market for a man at the moment—however gorgeous.' Then she turned the subject on to clothes and the conversation went safely on until Julia yawned and said that jet lag had caught up with her and she was going to bed.

'We've decided to take a bus into the city centre tomorrow to do some shopping,' she told Lyn. 'How about coming along?'

'Thanks, I'd like that.'

They arranged to meet in the foyer at two the next day and parted in the lift, Lyn going to her room very content with the way things were progressing.

Julia had three of the other stewardesses with her when Lyn kept her appointment the following afternoon. She was introduced to them as Netta Lewis and the five of them spent an enjoyable, giggly few hours looking for bargains among the chic clothes shops and

ending up in the famous Raffles Hotel for very English
tea and cakes.

Lyn tried to be as natural as she could, while at the
same time having to keep a guard on her tongue in
case she let slip anything that might give a clue to her
past. It was especially difficult to pretend to be ignor-
ant when the girls used flying jargon, such as referring
to foreign airports by their initials, and talking about
I.D. checks, reconciliations, briefings; all emotive
phrases that whisked Lyn back three years in time in
as many seconds.

Luckily they all seemed to have several things in
common, mainly the love of clothes, and Lyn was able
to change the subject when it looked like getting on to
dangerous ground, so the afternoon went very suc-
cessfully from her point of view. She found out that
two of the other stewardesses were dating men from
other airlines and didn't usually go out socially with the
rest of the crew unless it was something special like
someone's birthday. She also learnt that this was a long
lay-over for them in Singapore because they had three
whole days off, then took over from the crew of another
plane from London and went on with it to Jakarta, the
capital of Indonesia, and then to Bali where they stayed
overnight, doing the return trip the next day. They then
had another three days in Singapore before flying back
to London. This type of lay-over happened every third
trip and was very popular with most of the crew.

The girls squeezed into a taxi back to the hotel and
afterwards stood in the foyer, laughingly trying to work
out which parcels belonged to which girls. As they
stood there, two men walked into the hotel and Lyn
found herself face to face with Beric. She quickly
looked away and spoke to Julia, but was intensely aware

of him as he came over to their group with the other man, who she vaguely remembered being among the cockpit crew.

The second man spoke first. 'God, not more clothes! You girls go crazy every time you come over here. I don't know how on earth you manage to store them all, let alone wear them.'

Julia laughed. 'Oh, don't worry, we manage.' She turned to walk to the lifts, and Lyn, who had been pretending to concentrate on looking into one of her shopping bags, turned to follow her. But Beric's voice halted them.

'I see you've found a friend,' he remarked.

Julia turned back and Lyn reluctantly followed suit. 'Oh, I'm sorry,' Julia apologised. 'I should have introduced you. Netta, this is our Captain, Beric Dane, and our Flight Engineer, John Reese.'

Slowly Lyn lifted her eyes and found Beric looking at her, a lazy smile on his lean features, an appreciative look in his eyes as they ran over her. Not letting anything show on her face, she transferred her gaze to the other, older man, gave a small nod of greeting in their general direction and said coolly, 'How do you do?'

Surprise flickered in Beric's eyes for a second. He moved towards her and said, 'You look loaded down with parcels. Let me take some for you.'

Lyn replied shortly, 'I can manage, thank you,' and turned to walk with the other girls to the lifts.

Again the flicker of surprise showed in Beric's blue eyes, but he fell into step with her as they crossed the foyer. 'I haven't seen you here before, have I?' he asked. 'Which airline are you with?'

'I'm not with an airline, Mr Dane. I live in Singapore.'

The lift came and she nodded her thanks to the Flight Engineer as he stood aside to let her enter.

'Are you doing anything tonight, Netta?' Julia asked her as the lift rose. 'We thought of going to the night-club in the hotel, if you'd like to come along with us. I understand the singer there is quite good.'

'Yes, she is,' Lyn acknowledged. 'Thanks, I'd like to.'

The lift stopped at the seventh floor and the Flight Engineer, John Reese, said to her, 'Goodbye, Netta, nice to have met you.'

'Goodbye.' She turned to Beric. 'Goodbye.'

He paused in the doorway and turned. 'It's only au revoir; I'll see you in the night-club with the others tonight.'

As soon as the lift doors closed behind him the other girls broke into laughter.

'I knew he wouldn't be able to resist,' Julia gurgled. 'He doesn't usually get the icy reception that you gave him. I thought it would arouse his interest.'

'You mean you deliberately set this up?' Lyn demanded with pretended indignation.

'Of course,' Julia exclaimed. 'I knew that the first time he saw you he'd try to—er—how shall we put it? try to get to know you better.'

'Oh, did you? But I already told you that I'm off men.'

'You might think you are,' one of the other girls put in, 'but I've yet to see a woman who can resist Beric when he really puts himself out to make a conquest.'

'Well, let's hope Netta can,' Julia answered. 'It would be interesting to see our gallant Captain brought to heel.'

They reached Lyn's floor then and she said goodbye and stepped out, but as the doors closed behind her she heard one of the girls say, 'I wouldn't like to place any bets on her succeeding, though.'

Lyn dressed very carefully that evening, using all the make-up tricks that Nadia had taught her back in England, and putting on a very simple but elegant dove-grey dress with a scoop neckline, long sleeves and soft, floating full skirt. Her hair she had washed and brushed back, but into a softer style than she had worn during the day. Then she stood back and looked at herself critically in the full-length mirror. Yes, the dress gave the right effect, matching the grey lenses, and adding to the cool but sophisticated impression she wanted to make, but without adding the hardness that a strong colour might suggest.

Deliberately Lyn waited half an hour after the time she was supposed to meet the others and timed her entrance for when the group was between numbers and the floor was empty. She paused for a moment under the light just inside the doorway, tall and slender, her blonde hair shining like an aureole round her head. Julia and most of the crew were sitting together at a table on the far side of the night-club. They waved to her and a hush fell over the room as all heads turned to watch her cross the floor. As she neared the table all five men who were sitting there rose to their feet. Beric pulled out an empty chair beside him and the men in the room gave a soft sigh as they realised that she was with him.

Lyn sat down, her features composed, and was introduced to the other men in the party that she hadn't met before. They were the First Officer and the two stewards. The Navigational Officer, it seemed, had friends in Singapore he was visiting that evening.

After he had made the introductions, Beric turned to her. 'What can I get you to drink?'

'I'd like a gin and tonic, please.'

He called the waiter over and gave the order, then turned to speak to her again, but Lyn had started to talk to the girl sitting next to her and had her back half turned towards him.

He waited, making no attempt to claim her attention until the drink came, when Lyn had to look at him as she thanked him.

'Julia was telling us that you teach in a school here,' he remarked quickly before she could turn away again.

'Yes, that's right. I teach French and fill in when any of the other teachers are away.'

As she spoke a puzzled look came into his eyes, but Beric merely said, 'Have you been here long?'

'No, only a few weeks.'

'You won't have seen much of Malaya yet, then?'

'No, not a great deal, but I hope to take one or two trips during the Easter holidays.'

The band began to play a slow, smoochy number and Beric put his hand on her arm. 'Let's dance, shall we?'

Lyn could feel his fingers scorching into her flesh through the thin material of her sleeve. She thought about being held in his arms as they danced; her heart began to thump painfully and a wave of hatred filled her chest. Shortly, almost curtly, she answered, 'Not right now, thanks,' pulled her arm free and turned her back on him as she leant across the table to speak to Julia.

Four of the others went to dance, but fortunately everyone else stayed seated; Lyn had had a nightmare

vision of everyone else getting up to dance and leaving
her alone at the table with Beric. The talk became general again and then everyone sat and watched as the
singer came on for her first appearance. Afterwards
one of the stewards asked her to dance, and Lyn
accepted. He was quite good-looking, not completely
sure of himself with such a sophisticated girl, and Lyn
liked him, but she steadfastly refused when he asked
her for a date on the following night. When the dance
finished he led her back to her seat and said wryly to
Beric, 'She's all yours, Captain,' making it evident that
he thought she had refused him because she preferred
the pilot to the steward.

Lyn flushed slightly and Beric frowned, but Julia
hastily stepped into the little gap of silence and the
incident was immediately smoothed over. Lyn danced
with all the other men in the party before Beric asked
her again. It was a fast beat number this time, she
would be able to dance without him holding her, without having to touch him and feel his hands on her.
She nodded and stood up as he pulled her chair out for
her and preceded him on to the dance floor. He danced
well, moving in time to the music and not afraid to
loosen up, whereas Lyn moved woodenly, her legs
feeling like sticks as she longed for it to end. She tried
to keep her eyes on the other dancers, anywhere but
on Beric's face. When the music ended at last she gave
a small sigh of relief and went to move off the floor,
but the group almost immediately went into a slow
number and Beric put out an arm to stop her.

'Let's dance this one as well, shall we?'

Lyn stood transfixed as he put his arm round her
and drew her to him. Automatically she began to move
in time to the music and slowly raised her hand to his

shoulder. The other he took in his, lifting it against his chest, his clasp firm and strong. Lyn looked fixedly at his chest, the woody tang of his aftershave filling her nostrils, and felt as if she was going to faint. She remembered other times, other places, when he had held her just like this or even closer, as close as a man and a woman could get while they were dancing. Sudden desolation filled her heart and her hand began to shake. Above her head Beric said something, but she didn't hear him clearly.

Desperately she tried to take a hold of herself. 'I'm—I'm sorry, Mr Dane, what did you say?'

He looked down at her, a quizzical curl to his lips. 'Aren't you being rather formal—Miss Lewis?' he said mockingly.

Lyn grabbed at straws. 'I'm afraid I don't altogether approve of the current fashion of everyone being on first name terms the moment they meet,' she returned stiltedly. Beric frowned and she added, 'I see you don't agree.'

'What?' He seemed abstracted. 'Oh. Yes, I do to a certain extent.' He shook his head a little. 'I'm sorry, it's your voice. I'm sure I've heard it before somewhere. I thought so earlier on, but I simply can't remember where.'

CHAPTER FOUR

Lyn's heart froze. She hadn't given a thought to her voice. Oh, God, she thought, don't let him recognise it and see through me! For a moment her brain was paralysed as she wondered what on earth she was going to do. Too late to change her voice, she would have to go on with it, but what to say? In sheer desperation she arched her brows and said coldly, 'Well, I suppose that *is* a rather novel way of saying "Haven't we met before somewhere?" But not a very novel approach.'

Beric looked down at her under heavy lids. 'What is it with you, *Miss Lewis*? Why the cold shoulder treatment?'

Trying to keep her tone light, Lyn retorted, 'Your reputation has gone before you, Captain Dane. I don't like big bad wolves.'

He smiled sardonically. 'Afraid of getting eaten?'

'No, just of being mauled to death.' She drew away from him. 'Let's sit down, shall we?'

The eyes of the others rested on them speculatively as they returned to the table, but Lyn tried not to give anything away by her manner. Beric certainly didn't, casually lighting a cigarette and calling the waiter over to order another round of drinks.

Lyn picked up her bag. 'Oh, please, let me. I'm sure it must be my round.'

Reaching out a hand to stop her as she took out her purse, Beric said shortly, 'This is our party.' Then he added, with the first look of real warmth she'd seen in his eyes, 'But thanks for the offer.'

They broke up about one in the morning, by which time Lyn felt light headed from both tension and drink. She collapsed on to her bed, so enervated that she hardly had the strength to pull her clothes off and wash her face before she fell asleep.

The next day was Sunday and she slept late, but the shrill ring of the telephone beside her bed brought her startlingly awake in the morning, frightened because for a moment she thought she was back in prison where her life had been governed by harsh, strident bells. Quickly she grabbed the receiver off the rest to stop the noise.

'Hallo. Who is it?' she demanded, fear still in her voice.

'It's all right, Little Red Riding Hood,' Beric's voice, heavy with mockery, answered. 'The wolf is safely in his lair.'

'Oh! Oh, it's you.'

'As you so succinctly put it,' he agreed. 'How would you like to take a picnic and spend the day alone with me on a sailing boat in the Straits?'

'I wouldn't,' Lyn answered shortly.

Sounding quite unperturbed, Beric went on, 'Then how about joining the rest of my crew for a game of tennis followed by a dip in the pool over at the Country Club?'

Lyn thought about it. '*All* the crew?' she asked.

'All except the Navigational Officer, who won't be back until later.'

'I'll think about it,' Lyn said cautiously.

Beric laughed shortly, 'If you're thinking of checking with Julia, her room number's one-two-two-nine. See you in the lobby in an hour.'

Lyn did check with Julia, who laughed and said, 'Well, we've been *told* we're all playing tennis. What have you done to Beric, Netta? He doesn't usually bother to arrange things for us. He must really have accepted your challenge.'

'I didn't issue one,' Lyn informed her.

'Oh, yes, you did; the moment you said no when he asked you to dance, *and* when you came to sit down in the middle of a number. That kind of thing just doesn't happen to our revered Captain.'

There was a trace of irony in her voice and Lyn wondered briefly if Julia had ever made a play for Beric herself. Partly because of this she said earnestly, 'I meant what I said, Julia; I don't want to get involved with him or anyone.'

'But you'll come and play tennis?'

'Yes, I'd like to. It can be lonely here when you don't know anyone,' Lyn admitted.

Eight of them went to the Country Club in two taxis, Lyn being careful not to go in the same one as Beric. When they arrived Lyn found that he had not only booked a court, but had also hired a nearby cabana where they could go and shower and change. Having played a little tennis at the school, Lyn wasn't completely out of practice, but lost when she played with one of the stewards against Julia and John Reese, whereas Beric won his game easily. As Lyn sat in the lounger under the shade of one of the few palm trees left in Singapore, she watched him under half-closed lashes. He seemed to have lost none of his strength and fitness in the three years since she had known him, even though, if Julia hadn't exaggerated, he now spent most of his time wining, dining and bedding different women. But he hadn't had that sort of reputation

before, she thought musingly; that of an eligible bachelor who sometimes dated the stewardesses, yes, but
not as a flagrant womaniser.

He finished his match and walked over to where the
others were sitting, bending to pick up his towel and
rub himself down, then pulling the top off a can of
cold beer and raising it to his lips to drink thirstily.
Lyn watched him, the sun shining on the fine hairs on
his arms and at the V of his shirt, the beads of perspiration on his brow, and felt a strange prickling sensation in her fingertips.

Beric looked up and caught her watching him. His
mouth curved into a thin, sardonic smile, a knowing
look in his eyes. Lyn's hands quickly gripped the arms
of her chair tightly, and she suddenly realised what it
was about him that was different. It was cynicism. It
showed in his face, in the way his lip curled when his
smile didn't reach his eyes and the way he looked at
women, as if they'd been tried and found wanting. She
couldn't remember it being in his face before—but
perhaps she had just been too blindly in love to see it
there. It was surprising what a different complexion
hate could put on things.

Beric finished his beer and crossed to squat down on
the grass beside her. 'Are you going to play another
game?'

Lyn lay back and shook her head. 'No. One match
in this humidity is enough for me.'

'Come for a stroll in the gardens, then? It's cooler
there.'

'No, thanks,' she answered equably. 'I'm comfortable as I am.'

'One day,' he said with calm self-assurance, 'you're
going to say yes to me.'

'I doubt it.'

He smiled slightly, reached up to take her hand, and began to play with her fingers. Lyn tried to jerk free from his hold, but he wouldn't let go, instead bending to gently bite the soft mound of flesh near the base of her thumb, her mount of Venus.

'Don't pretend that you're not aware of me, Netta. We both know you are. You're as aware of me as I am of you.'

Her eyes widened as she glared at him indignantly, but he only raised his eyebrows quizzically, enjoying his domination over her, until he laughed and let her go.

They took it in turns to change into swimsuits, all the girls wearing bikinis except Lyn, who put on a cream one-piece costume. She also sat at the side of the pool, refusing to go in, luckily having remembered in time that she couldn't swim wearing contact lenses, and she certainly couldn't take them out! So she lay beside the pool and added a darker tone to her already golden tan.

After a few rapidly swum lengths Beric climbed out and stood looking down at her. He flicked some water over her and she opened her eyes and wrinkled up her nose at him. He laughed as if he meant it.

'Wake up, pussycat, lying there in the sun. Why don't you come in the pool?'

'I don't swim,' she lied, thinking that it was better that way.

'I'll teach you,' he offered.

Lyn shook her head.

'What's the matter, don't you trust me?'

Her voice dry, she answered, 'How did you guess?'

'You're quite wrong about me, you know. You'd be

quite safe in my hands. I wouldn't let any harm come to you,' he said softly, and Lyn suddenly knew that he wasn't talking about swimming at all.

After a moment she answered, 'I'm sure you'd very soon get bored with teaching me.'

'Not at all. I'm sure you'd make a very——' he paused, then added deliberately, 'rewarding pupil.'

'And when you fly away?'

'Well, if you couldn't wait for me to get back and give you more lessons, then I'm sure that what I'd already taught you would be extremely satisfying.' He said it with calm arrogance, sure that she was only putting up a token resistance that he would soon break down.

Lyn looked up at him for a long moment, then said coldly, 'I've already told you—I don't swim,' and turned her head away.

She continued to say no for the rest of that evening and all the next day too. No when he asked her out to dinner, no when he invited her on a trip out to Pasir Panjang to see the Tiger Balm Gardens, and definitely no when he suggested she fly out with the crew to Bali the next day and stay there overnight.

They left in the middle of the afternoon and Lyn went along with them to the airport to see them off, the thought always in the back of her mind of the day when she would slip the heroin into Beric's hand baggage. But it had to become natural for her to go with them and see them off first. By this time, when Beric looked at her there was a frown in his eyes, the more so because all the crew knew that he was getting nowhere with her. At the airport she met the elusive Navigational Officer, Tony Trent, who was about thirty, quite good-looking and full of fun. Lyn pretended to like him and laughed at his jokes, but they had only been talking for a few minutes when Beric broke it up by saying it was time they left.

While they were away a beautiful bouquet of flowers arrived for her, and Lyn hardly had to look at the card to know they were from Beric. The gift made her pause and she sat on her bed for a long time, gazing at the flowers and trying to think things out. It was true that her reason in coming to Singapore was to get close to Beric, but she had never stopped to think about how close and how quickly. She had only wanted to get near enough to find out if he was dope smuggling or to plant some on him, the latter probably being the easier, but she had based her plans on his character as she had known it, when he had taken time to get to know her and hadn't rushed her at all. But now the difference in his character worried her; she was afraid that if she said no for too long he would give up on her entirely, but there was no way she was going to say yes to going out with him if it also meant going to bed with him. No way could she stomach that; even to have him touch her made her flesh burn, her brain fill with hatred. At length she decided that for the moment she would go on as she was. The gift of the flowers proved that he was far from giving up, so she would go on blowing cold and rely on her instincts to tell her whether or not to change.

There were flowers the next day too and he rang her in the evening as soon as he got back to the airport. Lyn told him she already had a date, which was true as she had been invited round to the home of a fellow teacher to dinner, but she didn't tell Beric that, of course.

When she got back to the hotel he was waiting in the foyer.

'Hallo. How about a nightcap before you go up?'
Lyn hesitated, but he said sardonically, 'There are still
plenty of people in the bar.'

'All right.' She let him put a hand under her elbow
and lead her to an empty booth.

He ordered the drinks, lit a cigarette and looked
across at her frowningly. 'Enjoy your date?'

'Yes, thank you,' Lyn returned coolly.

Her aloofness seemed to annoy him, but he kept the
conversation impartial, putting himself out to charm
her and draw her out. Lyn sat back and enjoyed the
act, knowing it to be nothing more, and obligingly
smiled and laughed as if she was a member of an audi-
ence. After two more drinks he suggested a stroll in
the garden to get a breath of air, and could hardly
hide the gleam of triumph in his eyes when she
agreed.

The garden had a terrace looking towards the city,
and they could see the lights of the harbour with its
profusion of shipping, and the tiny moving lights that
seemed to be suspended in mid-air which came from
the cable cars that ran over the waters of the harbour
from Mount Faber to the island of Sentosa.

'Have you been up in the cable cars yet?' Beric asked
her.

Lyn shook her head. 'No, but I intend to go with
Julia and the girls some time.'

'Why not come with me?' He put his hands on her
waist and turned her round to face him. His eyes were
very intense as he drew her slowly towards him. 'Netta,
you're so lovely,' he breathed. 'So very beautiful.'
Bending his head, he gently touched her bare shoulder
with his lips. 'Do you know what you're doing to me?'
His mouth travelled along the line of her shoulder,

began to kiss her neck. 'Don't tease me any more, darling. We could have such a wonderful time together if only you'd stop playing games.'

He drew her close to him, so that she could feel his lean hardness against her. She remembered another hotel garden long ago and a quiver of emotion ran through her. Beric felt it and mistook it for desire. His voice thick, his lips against her throat, he said, 'Oh God, Netta, you're so beautiful, so desirable.'

His lips sought hers and he began to kiss her with a passion that slowly died as he realised that she wasn't responding, was standing woodenly in his arms. Slowly he lifted his head and looked at her.

Clearly, emotionlessly, Lyn said, 'You're mistaken, I'm not playing a game. I said no and I meant it. I don't want to go to bed with you and I won't! Just because you regard yourself as some sort of flying stud it doesn't mean that I have to want you, does it? And I certainly don't intend to become just another notch on your gun!'

Her voice had risen in anger and now she pushed herself free of him and ran back through the gardens towards the hotel, leaving him looking after her with a stunned expression on his face.

The next day she didn't see Beric at all, but in the afternoon went shopping with Julia, who immediately demanded to know what had happened between them. 'You must have done something to him,' she said. 'He went off like a bear with a sore head this morning and nearly snapped our heads off; gave us hell for talking about him behind his back.'

'I think I finally got it across to him that I wasn't interested, that's all.' And when Julia pressed her for details Lyn added, 'I'd really rather not talk about it.

But I'm sorry if you got into a row.'

'Oh, think nothing of it,' Julia answered. 'I'm enjoy-ing the whole thing.' She shivered dramatically. 'I wonder what he'll do next?'

So did Lyn wonder, with some trepidation, but Beric didn't put in an appearance the next day either and she began to be frightened that she'd gone too far, but on the third and last day of their lay-over he suddenly turned up in the foyer as they were leaving to play tennis at the Country Club again. He greeted her coolly and made no attempt to sit next to her in the taxi or at the Club. The others all tried to behave naturally, but there was a tension in the air that was impossible to dispel.

When they went swimming Lyn again sat out, but they all looked so cool, splashing about and playing ball in the water, that it only made her feel hotter and stickier, so she went into the cabana to shower. After-wards she was drying herself, her hair hanging loose on her shoulders, and had put on her brief bikini pants when she heard the door of the cabana open behind her. Hastily she pulled the towel over her chest and turned, expecting to see one of the girls. But it was Beric who stood in the doorway, droplets of water running down his broad, hairy chest and dripping on the floor.

'Can't you knock?' Lyn demanded, hugging the towel closer to her.

'Sorry. Julia wanted her towel.' He pushed the door shut and looked round. 'Which one is it?'

'The blue one. Now will you please get out of here?' she ordered.

An angry light came into Beric's eyes and his jaw tightened. 'Not until I'm good and ready.' He came over to her and Lyn hastily turned her back. 'What is it with you, anyway?'

Lyn didn't answer, just stood there, her heart thumping, feeling strangely nervous, something telling her that the next few minutes could be crucial.

'Netta?'

She could feel his breath on her hair, feel the heat of his body close to her back.

Gently he reached out and touched the scar on her hip where she'd fallen off her bicycle as a child, then his hand covered her hipbone, began to caress her, his other hand coming to cover the other side.

'No!'

But she mightn't have spoken. His hands moved up to span her waist, carried on up. Lyn began to tremble violently. Her skin felt burning hot and she could hardly breathe.

'Don't!'

But he was pulling the towel away and his hands were at her breasts, touching, caressing, becoming urgent as he pulled her back against his bare, wet chest.

'Oh God, you're driving me mad! I want you so much. Netta, darling.' He turned her round and pulled her hard against him, his mouth taking hers hungrily, compulsively.

'No! Stop it!' Lyn put her hands against his chest and tried to push him away, but her struggles only made him hold her tighter.

'Stop fighting me. You want this as much as I do. You tremble every time I touch you.'

'No! Let me go!'

There was real panic and hatred in Lyn's voice as he tried to kiss her again. Getting a hand free, she desperately slapped him across the face, so hard that it hurt her palm. Beric's head jerked back and his grip eased enough for her to break free. Shaking with anger and emotion, she grabbed up the towel and quickly covered herself again.

'Now get out of here!' she yelled at him, her voice close to hysteria.

Beric glared at her, his eyes pale blue with rage, his cheek already turning red where she'd hit him. He opened his mouth to say something and took a step towards her, but Lyn backed away, and shouted, 'Men are all the same! All you ever think about is sex!'

His lip curled derisively. 'Maybe you haven't heard—men aren't the only ones who enjoy sex nowadays, women get a kick out of it too! Just because you're getting over a love affair that went wrong, it doesn't mean that . . .'

Lyn interrupted him fiercely. 'I have *not* had an affair!'

'No?' His tone was infinitely sarcastic. 'Well, romance, or whatever you care to call it.'

'I don't care to call it anything,' she retorted furiously. 'I don't have affairs.'

'So why tell Julia that you were off men unless you'd just broken up with someone?' he demanded, his voice as hot with anger as her own.

Lyn glared at him, cornered, and seeking for a lie to back up the earlier one. Instinct, backed up by truth, made her say unevenly, 'Because they're all like you. All they want to do is get you into the nearest bed, and they won't take no for an answer. It doesn't matter to them that you have principles, that you want to lead a clean and decent life until the right . . .' She broke off, bit her lip and turned her head away. 'Oh, what's the use? Just go away and leave me alone!'

Beric was staring at her incredulously, an amazed look in his blue eyes. 'What are you trying to tell me?'

'I'm not trying to tell you anything! Will you please get the hell out of here so that I can get dressed?'

But before she realised what he was doing, he had crossed to her, put his hand on her chin and forced her to face him. 'Are you saying that you've never been to bed with a man? That you're still a virgin?'

Lyn stared up at him, chest heaving, her breathing uneven. Suddenly her eyes filled with tears and she looked away. 'Get out of here,' she gasped on a sob. 'Do you hear me? Get out!'

Slowly Beric took his hand away, still staring at her, then he turned abruptly, picked up Julia's towel from where it had fallen, and walked out of the cabana, slamming the door shut behind him.

Lyn leant back against the cool wall, eyes shut, feeling sick inside and wondering what on earth she'd done. Had she blown it, ruined all her carefully made plans because she'd got angry when he handled her? She remembered the feel of his hands on her breasts and she shuddered. Maybe she shouldn't have slapped his face like that, but she just couldn't bear to have him touch her a moment longer. Aware that the other girls might come into the cabana at any minute, she slowly finished dressing and did her hair and make-up, the latter difficult because her hand was still shaking. When she'd finished she gathered up her things and hesitated by the door, not knowing how to go out there and face him, or the others, who were bound to have guessed that something had happened even if they hadn't heard them shouting. Then she recalled the way she'd felt the day she was taken to Holloway Prison and had walked through the gates. This ordeal was nothing compared to what that had been. Putting on her dark glasses, Lyn squared her shoulders and walked out into the sun.

Relief flooded her as she saw that Beric, and all the men, weren't there. Julia told her that they'd gone over to the bar for a game of billiards and looked at her expectantly. 'Come on, give,' she commanded. 'What were you two rowing about?'

Lyn flushed. 'So you heard?'

'The whole pool heard. What was it about?'

'I objected to him coming in without knocking.' She looked at the other girl narrowly. 'But now I come to think of it he was at the other end of the pool when I went in to change and may not have known I was in there. And I wouldn't put it past you to have sent him in the cabana for your towel on purpose. Did you?'

Julia grinned. 'Well, we're leaving tomorrow, so I thought perhaps I'd stir things up a bit.'

'It did,' Lyn admitted with feeling.

'So how did it end?' one of the other girls demanded.

Lyn shrugged. 'How do you think? I shouldn't think either of us will ever speak to the other again.'

And when the men eventually came back, Beric hardly looked at her. He was morose and taciturn, impatient to leave the Club and only stopping to pay off the taxi before nodding curtly at them all and striding off by himself. He didn't join them that evening either, and his manner was still withdrawn the following afternoon when Lyn walked down to the hotel lobby with the girls to see them off to the airport. She thought that in the circumstances it would be better if she didn't travel in with them this time.

Beric saw her, looked away, and then turned back again, his brows drawn into a frown. For a moment their eyes held, then Lyn flushed and lowered her head.

'Here's the bus,' Julia announced. ' 'Bye, Netta, see you in ten days' time.'

The others echoed her goodbyes and Lyn went out to wave to them as the bus pulled away. Beric gazed at her through the window for a few seconds, then abruptly turned his back as the bus drove out of the forecourt.

CHAPTER FIVE

FOR the next ten days Lyn lived in an agony of suspense as she waited for the crew to return. No flowers arrived now and the others soon died in the heat. Lyn looked at the drooping heads and wondered if it had all been for nothing: the changes to her face, the contacts, the time, the money, all of it. Slowly she dropped the poor dead things into the waste paper basket and wondered for the ten thousandth time whether she'd ruined everything.

Unfortunately on the day they were due to fly in, she had to work at the school in the afternoon, taking the place of one of the teachers who had to go to the dentist, so she didn't see them arrive. Back at the hotel she hesitated by the phone, wondering whether to call Julia, but then decided to shower and change first. But she'd hardly slipped off her dress before there was a knock at the door.

'Just a minute.' Lyn slipped on an ivory silk full-length housecoat and opened the door.

Beric stood there, still in his uniform, his face grim. Lyn took one look at him and tried to slam the door, but he put his arm up to stop her and easily shouldered it open again. Then he stepped inside and pushed the door shut as Lyn backed away, her hand to her throat.

'I want to talk to you,' he said forcefully.

Lyn stared at him, frightened by his manner, her heart thumping in the sudden fear that he might have somehow found out the truth, knew who she was and what she planned for him. She tried to speak but couldn't, could only watch him as he looked round the room and then moved to the window. For all his forcefulness he, too, didn't speak at once, but stood looking out of the window for a moment before turning back towards her, his eyes running over her and settling on her face.

'What—what do you want?' Lyn managed, her voice dry in her throat.

He straightened up and said deliberately, 'I want you to have dinner with me tonight.'

Immediately a great rush of thankfulness filled her and she had to turn away quickly so that he wouldn't see it in her face. But he mistook her action for anger.

'You don't have to be afraid; there won't be any strings,' he added harshly.

Schooling her features as best she could, Lyn slowly turned to face him. 'Just exactly what does that mean?'

'What I said. I promise not to make any more passes at you.'

Her mind clicking like mad as she sought to work out how to play it, Lyn said warily, 'Why the sudden volte-face?'

'Do we have to have a debate about it?' He took three strides across the room and reached the other wall, turned impatiently and gestured with his hands. 'Let's just say that I thought about it in the time I've been away and found that I wanted to see you again. So I'm here—on your terms.'

'I wasn't aware of having made any terms.'

'Maybe you weren't, but you certainly laid them on the line.'

Lyn gazed at him uneasily for a minute, lips slightly parted, then she turned and walked over to the dressing table, picked up a hairbrush and put it down again. When she lifted her head she saw that he was watching her in the mirror. 'How do I know I can trust you?' she demanded bluntly.

'Because I give you my word,' Beric answered curtly, adding, when he saw the flash of disbelief in her eyes, 'And if you won't take that, then you'll just have to find out for yourself.' There was anger in his face from her unspoken insult and for a few moments she gazed at his reflection, wondering what to do.

'I—I don't know,' she said at length, looking away. 'I'll have to think about it.'

Immediately he crossed the room and caught hold of her by the shoulders, turning her round to face him. 'There's nothing to think about,' he said harshly. 'You either want to go out with me or you don't. You can give me your answer here and now.'

Lyn knew, then, that she had no choice. The time for playing hard to get had passed. If she said no now he would walk out of the room and she would never see him again, never have another chance to get near enough to him for her purpose.

Her voice strange and uneven, she raised her head to look into his taut, intent face and said, 'All right, I'll—I'll go out with you.'

His fingers had tightened on her shoulders, hurting her, but now he relaxed and let go, a strange look on his face as he straightened up. 'I'll come for you at seven. Wear something dressy.' At the door he paused for a moment to look back at her, nodded once as if satisfied, then left.

Her mind in a whirl, Lyn changed into a black lace dress with matching long-sleeved jacket and waited nervously for him to call for her, checking her hair and make-up in the mirror half a dozen times until she irritably realised that she was behaving like a schoolgirl on her first date. At ten to seven Julia rang and wanted to know if she felt like going down to the night-club.

'Thanks, Julia, but I already have a date tonight,' Lyn told her.

'How about tomorrow, then?'

'I'm not sure. Can I let you know?'

'Of course. Who is he? Someone special?'

Lyn laughed mirthlessly. 'I suppose you could say that.' Then she hurriedly finished the conversation before Julia could get too curious and guess the true situation.

His knock came promptly at seven; trust a pilot to be punctual! But Lyn waited until his second, impatient rap before she opened the door. Beric didn't smile, but his brows flickered as they ran over her. He was wearing a black evening suit and looked extremely big and handsome, his tan accentuated by the stark whiteness of his shirt.

His voice sounding strange, he said, 'You look—very lovely.'

'Thank you.' Lyn's tone, in answer, was cool, almost aloof.

'Are you ready?'

She nodded, picked up her evening bag and key and let him shut the door for her. He didn't speak or touch her as they walked to the lifts, but when one came he put a proprietorial hand under her elbow as he helped her in and kept it there. Many heads turned to look at them as they walked through the foyer, and Lyn caught a glimpse of themselves in one of the big mirrors. They made a handsome couple, both tall and tanned, the vitality of youth in their faces and the way they walked. And both good-looking; Beric because nature had made him that way, and Lyn because hate had impelled her to do something she would otherwise never even have contemplated.

Somewhat to her surprise, he took her to a concert by Singapore's Philharmonic Orchestra, which ordinarily Lyn would have enjoyed. But tonight she hardly heard the music, she was too aware of Beric sitting beside her, of the closeness of his arm to hers. He, too, seemed tense. Once or twice Lyn caught him watching her, but when they went for a drink in the interval he talked perfectly naturally, telling her about places he'd been to in the course of his flying career. That he should mention Miami was inevitable, but Lyn managed not to betray anything and put in a question that led him on to a different part of the world.

After the concert he took her to Fatty's Restaurant in Albert Street, which, in a city where every single person considered himself a gourmet, had a tremendous reputation and was always fully booked. But although Lyn appreciated the food, she found that she could only pick at it. She tried to keep up her end of the conversation, but her tenseness and nervousness showed through. At length they left and Beric called a taxi to take them to the hotel. Lyn sat stiff and silent in her corner, and Beric too was silent until he moved his arm and she instinctively jerked away.

'For God's sake relax,' he said harshly. 'I'm not going to eat you.'

'I—I know. I'm sorry.'

He reached out and took her hand and this time she managed to control herself and not draw away.

Back at the hotel he took her straight up to her room, took her key from her and opened the door, then handed it back to her.

'Tomorrow?'

Lyn looked down at her bag. 'I have to work tomorrow.'

'All day?'

'No, only in the morning.'

'Then tell me where your school is and I'll pick you up there so that we can spend the rest of the day together.'

'No,' Lyn said quickly, adding, 'I—I'd rather come back here first to shower and change.'

'All right. Phone me as soon as you're ready. I'm in room six-one-five this trip.'

She nodded, then said uncertainly, 'Goodnight,' not sure whether she ought to shake his hand, let him kiss her, or what.

For almost the first time that evening he smiled. 'Goodnight, Beric,' he ordered.

Lyn flushed. 'Goodnight—Beric.'

'That's better.' He put a hand up to her cheek, gently ran his finger over it as his eyes grew serious again, then he turned on his heel and walked quickly away down the corridor. When he was out of sight Lyn put up a hand and rubbed at her cheek where he'd touched it as if he'd left a dirty mark on her pale skin.

The next day they were both more at ease, Lyn having got over most of her nervousness about being with him, and Beric once again confident and self-assured. For lunch, he took her to the old Telok Ayer Market just off Raffles Quay, which used to be one of Singapore's main markets but which had now been cleaned up and contained about a hundred eating stalls where you could get Chinese, Indian, Malay and the local Nonya dishes as well as European hot dogs and hamburgers. It was incredibly noisy and full of people, but it was fun to perch on a three-legged stool and have your first course at a Malay stall and then move on to a Chinese one for the second.

Afterwards they walked up through the crowded, colourful streets of Chinatown where stallholders shouted their wares under the partial shade of huge umbrellas and brightly coloured awnings. From the houses on both sides of the street bamboo poles hung with washing stuck out from all the windows on all the storeys and there was constant danger of being dripped on unless you walked down the middle of the street. Lyn found the place exotic and fascinating; she would never have dared to venture there alone, but Beric was always there to protect her from being jostled and he rescued her from importunate sellers when she stopped to admire something.

From there they took a taxi to the House of Jade and walked into its cool interior to spend a couple of hours admiring the collection of beautifully carved pieces that dated from 206 B.C. Until recently jade was believed to have healing and calming properties as well as having the power to repel evil, so there were many rings, earrings and bracelets that the superstitious had once worn.

By the time they came out they were thirsty, so they went in the nearest bar to drink tall glasses of Singapore Gin Sling, a cocktail that had originated in the Raffles Hotel. Beric talked to her a lot now, smiling and laughing, completely at ease. But it was different from when he had tried to impress her on his previous lay-over; then he had been consciously putting himself out to attract her and, to her prejudiced eyes, it showed, but now he was completely natural and seemed to enjoy being with her, talking to her. Lyn deliberately tried to relax, to behave as she would have done if she had really been the girl she was pretending to be, and, strangely, she didn't find it too difficult, although sometimes she would stop short as she caught herself turning a laughing, glowing face up to Beric and seeing the answering gleam in his blue eyes. Then she would become withdrawn again for a while as she remembered that he had looked at her like that once before, and that she must be constantly on her guard against him, against his alert intelligence which would immediately fasten on any slip she might make, and against his dominant masculinity which had captured her and made her love him once before.

The next day she insisted on spending the morning with Julia and a couple of the other girls in the modern shopping centre, but told them that she had a date for the afternoon. They tried to get out of her who it was, but Lyn was vague, letting them think it was someone from the school. Julia told her that Beric had gone off the moment they had arrived in Singapore and they hadn't seen him since. 'He's probably found himself a new woman. It's a shame, Netta. We really thought your hard-to-get line would intrigue him.'

Lyn smiled, wondering what their reactions would be when they finally found out that they'd been right all along.

That day Beric hired a car, a convertible, and drove out first to the Japanese Gardens at Turong, where all the trees and walks were set out in an ancient traditional pattern, and where red-painted bridges spanned lakes and streams. As they walked the skies started to darken to a blackish hue as thunderheads started to build up, blotting out the sun and reminding Lyn suddenly of England in December. They just had time to make the shelter of an ornate pagoda before the rain fell from the sky in heavy, torrential drops. The air grew cold as lightning split the darkness and the thunder reverberated above them. Lyn shivered, and Beric slipped off the lightweight jacket he was wearing and put it round her shoulders. Then he put his arm round her and drew her to him. Lyn stiffened, but he did nothing more and she gradually relaxed, leaning against him.

They didn't talk much in the half hour that the storm lasted; Beric lit a cigarette and they watched the sudden violent eruption of nature as the lightning outlined the statues and pagodas in the gardens. Then it ended as suddenly as it had begun, the sun coming out and the stormclouds evaporating away, leaving that sickly sweet smell of damp grass and earth steaming in the heat.

Afterwards they went to the Orchid Gardens on the Mandai Lake Road, and Lyn exclaimed with delight at the fields of cultivated orchids in the most beautiful colours, their scent blown towards them by the breeze from the sea. Beric bought her a spray of them and pinned it to her dress so that the scent filled her nostrils every time she turned her head. He smiled at her as he pinned it on and she smiled back. For a moment his fingers became still, his eyes, as blue as the sky, looked at her intently, but then he went on with his task and the moment passed.

They dined at a small restaurant by the coast that specialised in the most delicious seafood, then Beric drove back into the city and parked near the cable car tower just as the sun was beginning to set. They went up in the lift and had a car to themselves as it began the slow ride two hundred feet above the waters of the harbour. Out to sea Lyn could see thunderclouds building up across the smaller islands, creating great purple, crimson and flame splashes of colour against the deep richness of the sunset. She drew a long breath of wonder. 'Oh, it's beautiful. So very beautiful.'

Beric nodded. 'I've seen plenty of sunsets, in a lot of distant places, but none were like this.'

They continued to watch until the cable car dropped too low and deposited them, with a little hiccup, at the terminal on the island of Sentosa. They wandered round the little island until it became dark, enjoying the refreshing breeze that blew from the South China Sea, and then took the cable car back again. This time there were none of nature's pyrotechnics to wonder at, but instead there were the man-made illuminations of the city spread out below them. The night was warm like the caress of velvet and the moon hung low in the sky so that Lyn felt as if she could reach out and touch it. It felt so strange to be in the little car, suspended in the air, almost as if she was suspended in time as well.

She turned to Beric and smiled. 'I feel as if this isn't real.'

He reached out and took her hand, his eyes searching her face. Then he raised his other hand and gently cupped her chin. Lyn's eyes must have widened, because he said quickly, 'It's all right, this isn't a pass. I'm going back to England tomorrow and I don't want to say goodbye to you with all the crew looking on.' He moved his hand so that his finger could trace the outline of her lips, very slowly and gently. His eyes, shadowed by the moonlight, studied each feature of her face as if he wanted to imprint every detail on his mind, then he said her name, his voice rough, unsteady, and slowly bent to kiss her.

Lyn could feel her heart pounding as his lips moved against hers, hard, compelling, and yet gentle too. It was different from the way he had kissed her before, in the cabana and the garden of the hotel. There had been arrogance in those kisses and demand, but now there was warmth and tenderness with passion and desire held back in subjugation. His lips caressed her mouth, as if he was delighting in its sweetness, exploring it with little intoxicating kisses that made her heart start to race.

'Netta. Oh, Netta, you're so lovely.' He breathed her name against her lips, murmured endearments as his mouth left hers and he began to kiss her throat, her eyes.

Lyn moved away from him suddenly, leant back against the cable car in a shaft of moonlight, her breathing unsteady, her lips parted as she stared at him, eyes wide.

Beric didn't try to come after her, just sat back in his seat, then reached into his pocket and fumbled for a cigarette, lit it and drew hard on it so that the end glowed like a bright star in the darkness. He turned to look at her. 'You'll come out with me on my next layover?' he said abruptly. It was a demand more than a question.

Lyn hesitated for a moment, then nodded. 'Yes.'

They were silent on the drive back to the hotel and he didn't try to kiss her at her door, just said a brief goodnight and walked away without looking back.

Two days later he phoned her from London. He talked about the flight for a while, then asked, 'When does the school break up for Easter?'

'On Friday. We have three whole weeks.'

'Have you made any plans?'

'Not really. One of the other teachers is thinking of taking a trip into the mainland and going up to Pahang and Cameron Highlands, and she asked me to go with her. But she isn't quite sure whether she can make it yet.'

Beric rang off soon after, but he phoned her every night that week. Probably to check on whether she had a date, Lyn thought cynically, but it was encouraging and proved he was still interested. Then one night he didn't phone, and her thoughts and hopes were immediately in chaos again.

The next day was Friday and her last at the school before the Easter holidays. She had stayed late to help close the place up and didn't get back to the hotel until nearly six o'clock, feeling hot and tired and longing for a shower. She took her key, walked across to a lift, and then stared as she turned round and found that Beric had walked in after her.

'But I—I thought you weren't due back for another five days?' she exclaimed.

'I wasn't. I had some leave due to me and decided to spend it here. I've got three weeks.' He smiled down at her, amusement in his blue eyes as he watched her surprised face.

'Oh,' she said inadequately, realising that he intended to be with her all through her holiday.

He walked along with her to her room and, as soon as they had stepped inside, shut the door and gently but firmly pushed her back against it. Then he kissed her long and lingeringly, as if he had been wanting to do it very much. At last he raised his head and sighed. 'I needed that.'

Lyn blinked at him and suddenly they were both laughing.

'Come on, woman, hurry up and get changed.' He pushed her towards the bathroom and gave her a light tap on the bottom as she passed. 'Tonight we're going out to celebrate.'

Lyn laughed as she closed the louvred door and began to undress. 'What are we celebrating?'

'The fact that we've got three whole weeks together, of course. Can I use your phone?'

'Go ahead.'

When she came out of the shower in her bathrobe, there was champagne waiting in a bucket of ice. They had a glass each and then Beric went out on the balcony to wait while Lyn changed.

'Right, you can come back in now,' she called as she went back into the bathroom to put on her make-up and do her hair.

He was lying on the bed, a glass of champagne in his hand, when she came out, and for a moment he didn't get up, just lay and looked at her. Then he put down the glass and got to his feet.

'Did I ever tell you that you're very beautiful?' He grinned wryly. 'But I suppose you're used to it by now.'

Lyn shook her head slowly. 'No, I'm not used to it. What I look like—outside, doesn't really matter to me.'

His eyes widened incredulously, then he said on a note of wonder, 'I really think you mean that.'

'Why shouldn't I?'

'Most girls care about nothing else but their appearance. And they'd give anything to have a face like yours.'

Abruptly Lyn turned away. 'Let's go, shall we?'

Beric was in a very happy, lighthearted mood that night, and Lyn—with the help of the champagne—found it not too difficult to match it. They had a meal and then went to a night-club in one of the other hotels, where they danced until the small hours. That evening he did kiss her goodnight, and repeated it more often as they spent their days together, exploring Singapore Island or just lazing under the sun on a beach or by the hotel pool.

Lyn let him kiss her, feeling that she couldn't hold him off completely, but she gave him no encouragement to go farther. She was sure in her own mind that he had only adopted this 'hands off' approach because he was piqued by her treatment of him, and that for all his promises not to make a pass his intention was still to get her to sleep with him. She thought that as soon as he felt sure enough of her he would again try to make love to her, and this time probably wouldn't take no for an answer. As she saw the situation, her only difficulty was going to be in holding him off until the end of the three weeks when he flew back to London. For a while she had toyed with the idea of planting some dope on him at the end of his leave, but had decided that it would be better if he carried it when he was actually flying the plane. Also it might be difficult to obtain the heroin when Beric was constantly with her. Singapore was one of the cities in the world that had a high number of drug addicts among its population, especially among the young—although it had made tremendous strides in dealing with the problem—and Lyn, through a contact she had made in prison, had already found out how she could get the amount she wanted. She had even obtained an identical carton of talcum powder to the one that had been planted on her which she intended to use, and which would leave Beric in no doubt whatsoever about who had turned the tables on him and why. So her only problem now was to keep him at arm's length until after this leave and his next lay-over, which, with a man of Beric's sexual appetite, wasn't going to be easy.

But to her surprise he didn't attempt to take things farther than kissing, possibly because it was always a case of *him* kissing her; she would let him do what he wanted, but she never responded, never touched him or gave any sign that his kisses aroused her in any way. His blue eyes then would grow bleak, shadowed, for a while, but he would determinedly throw it off until the next time he kissed her.

It was difficult to know how far to go or not to go. Lyn didn't want him to think that she was completely frigid and yet she still wanted to hold him off. They were sunbathing by the pool at the Country Club one afternoon when an opportunity came to give him a reason for her coolness.

'Why won't you come into the pool?' he asked her. 'Surely you trust me enough now not to let you drown?'

Lyn shook her head. 'It's not that. I'm afraid of the water. Somebody pushed me in when I was little and I nearly drowned. I haven't been able to go near it ever since,' she told him, inventing rapidly and feeling rather pleased with her explanation.

She had her hair down and Beric wound a lock of it idly round his finger. It lay gold and glistening against the brownness of his hand. 'You know, I seem to have told you an awful lot about myself, but I know hardly anything about you. Tell me about yourself,' he commanded.

Lyn smiled slightly, but her mind was racing, trying to think back three years to what she might have told him then. 'Oh, I've led a very boring life. There's really nothing to tell. Whereas you . . .'

'Tell me anyway,' Beric interrupted peremptorily.

Her voice cautious, she said, 'What do you want to know?'

'Everything. Every detail from the moment you were born. I want to know everything about you.'

Lyn looked at him quickly, surprised by the demand in his tone, then shrugged. 'All right. I'm twenty-two years old and I was born in Buckinghamshire.' Which was true. 'My parents died when I was quite young and I was sent away by my aunt to be educated in a convent school.' Which was completely untrue.

'A convent school? You're a Catholic?'

'No.' Lyn shook her head, her mind racing ahead. 'But my aunt had the school recommended to her, so I was sent there.'

'And after you left school?' Beric prompted.

'I went to a French convent for a few months to study the language, then went back to teach at my old school.'

Beric raised himself on his elbow to stare at her. 'You mean you've been stuck inside a convent nearly all your life?'

'Not a convent. A school run by nuns,' she corrected.

'There were no men there?'

Lyn laughed. 'Only the priests and the caretaker.'

'Good Lord! So how did you escape and get to Singapore?'

'My aunt died,' Lyn told him, glad to get at least halfway back to the truth again. 'She left me some money. At first I went to London, but ...' she shrugged, 'that didn't work out. Then I heard about this job and decided to come out here.'

'Why didn't London work out?'

Lyn looked away and didn't answer, but Beric sat up and leaned over her, his eyes studying her intently. 'Was it a man?'

Slowly she shook her head. 'Not any one man in particular. I went to a hair care and beauty course. They taught you how to dress, how to wear make-up, but they didn't teach you how to handle men. They seemed to think that you already knew all that. But I didn't—so I left, ran away, I suppose.'

Beric looked at her, his face tighter. 'That explains quite a bit.'

Lyn hoped it would, fervently. And it appeared to have worked, because Beric seemed to have become even more protective towards her, treating her almost like a fragile piece of porcelain that had just been taken off the shelf and has to be handled with delicate care. Which suited Lyn very well.

After a few days he suggested they fly up to Penang and spend the rest of their three weeks there.

'Penang? That's up in the north, isn't it?' Lyn asked, although she knew perfectly well where it was, but she wanted time to think.

'Yes, it's on the west coast, quite near the border with Thailand. It's an island, not unlike Singapore, but much quieter and a lot less people.'

They were strolling through the Botanical Gardens at the time and Lyn halted under the shade of a frangipani tree, the fragrant petals of its white flowers close above her head. She looked at Beric closely but could read nothing from his expression. 'Why do you want to go there?' she asked.

'To show you another part of the country that I think you'll like. To be in a quieter place together.'

Lyn reached up to pick one of the blossoms and looked at the delicate, translucent petals in her hand. 'Together?'

'I told you—there aren't any strings.' His voice sounded rough.

Lyn lifted her head to look at him steadily. 'Why now, Beric?'

'Now?'

'Yes. When the crew are due in tomorrow.'

He hesitated, then said, 'All right, I admit I'd rather not run into them.'

'I see.' Lyn threw down the petals angrily. 'I hadn't realised you're ashamed to be seen with me!' She turned sharply on her heel and began to hurry away from him.

'Netta! Wait!' Beric caught up with her in three strides and took hold of her arm, spinning her round to face him. 'Netta, that isn't so. Believe me.' He put his other hand on her free arm and gripped tightly, his voice urgent. 'If anything it's the other way round. I want it to go on like this, just the two of us. I don't want to share the time we have with other people, even the crew.' He smiled suddenly, his blue eyes laughing. 'And I definitely don't want to have the life teased out of me by Julia and the other girls. Not yet, anyway.'

Lyn looked at him uncertainly, trying to work it all out, from her own secret point of view as well as that of the part she was playing. Would he keep his word? Or would he try to coerce her into giving herself to him once he got her to Penang?

He took her silence for distrust and said rather heavily, 'Surely you know by now that I'll keep my word? That I won't try anything?' He put a finger under her chin. 'Trust me, little one,' he said softly.

Lyn had already made up her mind to go, but she let herself look into his eyes for a long moment before saying huskily, 'All right, I'll go with you.'

'That's my girl!' His eyes grew warm and he bent to gently kiss her on the lips.

Beric was right, she did like Penang. It was a beautiful jewel of a place with villages that looked as if they had been slumbering peacefully under the coconut palms for ever, with lovely, remote beaches, and cool green hills where you could look out across breathtaking panoramas of sea and coastline. They dined under the stars in an old fort that became a restaurant at night, and wended their way upwards through a warren of souvenir shops wedged on the shallow, steadily climbing stairs to the Million Buddahs Precious Pagoda which was set so high on a hilltop that it seemed to float in the clear blue air.

They did a lot and saw a great deal, and yet it seemed as if they had done everything very slowly; they didn't hurry and there was plenty of time to stroll hand in hand under a paradise of tropical trees, to stand and watch the fishing boats put out to sea, and to wait laughingly while a small bird picked out a fortune paper for them while its trainer cooed to it encouragingly. Beric's was very mundane: 'You are going to be lucky but you will have to work hard', while Lyn's read, 'A great change will come to you and you will travel far'.

'Well, the travel bit is right, anyway,' Lyn laughed.

'We go back to Singapore tomorrow.'

Beric took her hand and led her away from the market square down towards the ancient walls of Fort Cornwallis where they climbed the ramparts, and leaned against the warm, mellow old stones to watch the sunset. He didn't let go of her hand, but drew her to him so that she was half leaning against him.

'Maybe we could make the other half of your fortune come true as well,' he remarked.

'The great change bit?' Lyn looked up at him and saw the golden glow of the sunset reflected on his face. 'How?'

There was a tautness about his features as he lifted his hands to hold her arms and turn her completely round to face him. His voice slightly uneven, his eyes intense, he said, 'You could marry me.'

Lyn stared at him, completely stunned. 'M-marry you?'

'That's what I said,' he agreed, a slight curve of wry amusement on his lips now as he observed her reaction.

'But—but that's impossible! You can't mean it. But your sort don't . . .' She stopped abruptly, the sudden flare of anger in his eyes making her realise what she was saying.

'My sort!' he repeated harshly. 'Is that still how you look on me? As some sort of a rake? Do I have to go on treating you like a nun for the rest of my life just to prove to you that I'm not?'

'Don't! Please.' Lyn cut through his anger. 'I'm— I'm sorry. It's just that it was so unexpected. I just hadn't thought of you as the type to want to get married. I'm sorry,' she said again.

'You mean you haven't even thought about it, the

whole time we've been going out together?' he asked wonderingly. Adding, when she shook her head, 'Then just what did you think I was leading up to?'

Lyn shrugged and half turned away. 'I thought ... Well, people don't get married so much nowadays. They just live together. I thought that probably that was what you wanted. To live with me—while you were in Singapore on lay-overs.'

'Dear God!' He stared at her. 'And when I get put on to a different route?' he demanded harshly. 'What then?'

Lyn shrugged. 'Then it would be finished. You'd find someone else wherever you were flying to.'

'I see.' He laughed rather bitterly, and Lyn expected him to ask her whether she would have lived with him, but to her surprise he didn't. Instead he turned and gazed out over the ramparts, his mouth set into a hard, thin line. When he turned to look at her again there was a dejected look in his eyes. Rather tiredly he said, 'I suppose I've only myself to blame. If I hadn't tried to make you when we first met ...'

He paused and reached out for her, drew her back against him and held her there, gently running his hand up her bare arm. 'You see, I never expected to fall in love again. I never thought that I'd marry, and I admit that all I wanted women for was sex, and there were plenty of girls who were happy to provide just that.' His hand stopped for a moment, fastened on her arm. 'That's all I thought women were good for—until you. You made me realise that miracles can happen, that there's still a chance for love, a wife you can trust waiting for you when you get home, a family—all the things that I thought I'd never have. Netta,' slowly he turned her round to face him, 'I don't know the exact moment I fell in love with you; in some strange way it feels as if I've known you and loved you for a long time. And I do love you, darling, very much. You wouldn't have to worry—I'd never look at another woman, not now I've found you.'

Lyn turned her head away, avoiding his eyes. She felt strangely breathless, found it difficult to think straight, to work out how to use what had happened to her advantage. Partly to play for time, partly because she couldn't resist asking, she said slowly, 'You said you didn't expect to fall in love *again*. That must mean that you've been in love before?'

For a moment his hand tightened, then he let her go and straightened up. 'Once,' he admitted curtly. 'But it didn't work out.'

'What happened?'

'Nothing happened. I didn't play around with other women, if that's what you mean.' He thrust his hands deep into his pockets. 'I just found out in time that she didn't love me after all; love or trust me.'

'You were going to marry her?'

'That was the general idea.'

'I see.'

Beric turned to look at her, took her hand. 'No, you don't see, and I can't explain it all to you. But it was all over a long time ago, and, although it cut deep at the time, there's nothing left of it now. But I thought I was strictly a one-woman man and that I'd lost that one woman. Until now. You're the most wonderful thing that's ever happened to me, Netta. I love you, and I want you to be my wife.'

Lyn drew away from him and took a few agitated steps along the ramparts. She tried to think, but felt hopelessly confused. Somehow she ought to be able to use this situation, but she just couldn't think straight. Her only hope was to play for time. Her indecision showing in her voice and face, she said, 'I—I don't know. I've only known you a short time really. Okay, so we've been together these three weeks, but that doesn't mean that we'd be happy being together for the rest of our lives. I just don't know!' Beric took a step towards her and she rounded on him fiercely. 'And don't start giving me any ultimatums. No saying I either want to marry you or I don't and you want the answer here and now, like you did before. Because if you do then the answer's no! I refuse to be rushed.'

Beric lifted up his hands in a sign of peace. 'All right, you little spitfire! I won't coerce you—not tonight anyway. But that doesn't mean I'm not going to try and persuade you to make up your mind.' And he firmly took her in his arms and kissed her. When he at last let her go, he said thickly, 'Hurry up and say yes, darling. I can't wait to claim you as my own.'

The next day they flew back to Singapore and there was only time to have a meal together in the airport restaurant before Beric flew back to England. He held her very close as he said goodbye, his face buried in her hair, but he didn't say anything. He'd said everything there was to say the night before, and now he let the special light of love and tenderness in his eyes show her just how much she meant to him.

Lyn waited at the airport until his plane took off and disappeared from sight into the deep blue of the sky, then she turned and slowly walked out of the airport to get a taxi back to the hotel. There she lay on the bed for a long time, working things out, better able to think objectively somehow now that Beric was gone. Her first realisation was that he had handed her a weapon she had never even hoped to have. That he should admit that he loved her placed him immeasurably within her power; all she had to do was to find a way that that love could be turned on him to hurt him the most. The most obvious way was to just go ahead with what she had planned originally and let him know that she had done it and why. The fact that it was done to him by someone he loved being an added knifethrust. But somehow this didn't satisfy Lyn, she felt she could make better use of it than that. She thought of getting engaged to him and then having a blatant affair with another man. That would cut into his conceited arrogance all right! But it would also entail her having an affair with someone, and even the idea of that filled her with repugnance. She'd been through enough horrible experiences without having to do something hateful now—even if it meant getting her revenge on Beric.

Her mind still not made up, she went out for a meal and sat near some elderly people who were talking about a trip they had made that day out to Changi, the old prisoner-of-war camp where all the Europeans in Singapore had been held during the Japanese occupation. They then went on to talk about their experiences in London during the blitz when one of them had nearly been bombed. Lyn half-listened to them and it brought to mind a book she had once read about a man whose bride was killed by a bomb on their wedding night. She froze suddenly as an idea came to her and began to take shape in her mind, her eyes narrowing as she concentrated. Yes, of course. She wouldn't need the heroin after all. Why take the risk of being found with it in her possession when there was a much easier way of getting back at Beric, a way that would keep turning a knife in the wound for the rest of his life!

The next day she found a small, cheap flat in a high-rise block near the school and checked out of the hotel. If Beric wanted her that badly, then he would value her all the more if he had to fight to get her. She left her new address with the receptionist at the hotel and told him not to give it to anyone, but knowing full well that he was quite susceptible to a bribe.

On the day that Beric was due back she purposely stayed out late, first going shopping and then to a cinema. Back at the block of flats she took a lift to her floor and felt an immediate thrill of satisfaction as she saw him leaning against the wall by her door. He hadn't even waited to change out of his uniform, and looked as if he'd been there a long time. Hastily she put a look of surprise and fear on her face, and took a half step as if to get back in the lift. But Beric was beside her in two strides and had put a hand on her arm, holding her firmly.

'Where's your key?' he demanded curtly.

Her hands trembling with inner excitement, Lyn took it from her purse and gave it to him.

He pulled her inside the flat, shut the door with a slam, and then turned on her, his face furious. 'Why the hell did you move out of the hotel? I've been out of my mind with worry ever since I tried to phone you and they said you'd checked out. That was five days ago!'

Lyn carefully put down her shopping and moved away from him. 'How did you find me?'

'I got it out of the receptionist. Netta, why . . .'

But Lyn had swung round to face him. 'But I told him not to tell . . .' She broke off and bit her lip.

'So I gathered,' Beric said grimly. 'I had to threaten

to take him apart before he'd give it to me.'

Lyn's eyes widened; then she realised he must have been too angry to try bribery. Good, that meant his emotions were really aroused. She went to turn away again, but he caught her and made her face him.

'I asked you why you left the hotel!' he reminded her furiously.

Lyn lowered her head, acting for all she was worth, and filled with this strange, crazy inner excitement. 'It was too expensive,' she answered unevenly. 'I couldn't afford to stay there any longer.'

'Don't lie to me!' His voice was suddenly savage and he pushed her back against the wall. 'You were running away, without even a word to me. Weren't you? Weren't you?' he repeated furiously when she didn't answer at once.

'Yes, all right!' Lyn put her hands up as if to cover her ears from his fury. 'Yes, I was running away. Because I decided I didn't want to marry you, and I didn't—I didn't want to see you again.'

He was suddenly still, staring at her, his face white beneath his tan. 'So you just walked away,' he got out in little more than a hoarse whisper. 'Knowing how I felt about you—you just walked away!' He slammed his fist against the wall close to her head suddenly so that she jumped, then he swung away from her, fighting to gain control.

Making her voice tremble, Lyn said, 'Please try to understand. I *had* to leave like that. I wanted to make a clean break. I—I thought it would be better that way.'

'Better?' He jerked round to face her. 'Not knowing where you were or what had happened to you? I didn't even know the name of the school where you worked so that I could phone there!'

Lyn didn't answer, just stood looking at the floor, and at length he came over, his face very taut, his eyes bleak. Slowly he lifted his hands and put them on her shoulders. She could feel them trembling even through the layers of her clothes. It cost him an effort to control himself and his voice still sounded ragged as he said desperately, 'Why, Netta? Why won't you marry me?'

'I can't.'

'You're not in love with me?' The pain was raw in his voice.

'I just don't want to marry you, that's all,' she replied bluntly.

He winced as if she had hit him, but then his eyes widened as he realised that she hadn't denied that she loved him. Tersely he said, 'Why don't we sit down and talk it over?'

'There's nothing to talk about. I want you to go away. I don't—I don't want to see you again.'

'All right.' His voice was smooth now as he sensed her uncertainty, his anger gone and hope back in his eyes. 'But we don't have to part like this, do we? You could at least offer me a drink. I could do with one,' he said, and meant it.

'I'm—I'm sorry.' Lyn let herself be persuaded and moved to the tiny kitchen area. 'I'm afraid there's only the wine I was going to have with my meal.'

'That's fine.' He let her pour him out a glass, watching her narrowly all the time. 'Haven't you eaten yet? Go ahead and cook yourself something; don't let me stop you.'

Lyn looked at him uncertainly, then nodded. 'All right.' She picked up the shopping, then hesitated, not looking at him. 'Were—were you waiting long?'

'About three hours,' he answered steadily.

'Oh.' She looked quickly away. 'Then I expect you're hungry. Would you—do you want to eat here?'

'Thank you.' He tried to mask the quick gleam of triumph that came into the blue eyes.

Lyn cooked the meal and let him reluctantly draw her out while they ate, and then only made half-hearted attempts to get rid of him, finally letting him convince her that now he had found her they might at least be friends and spend the rest of his lay-over together.

He left about midnight in a far different frame of mind than he had arrived in, and Lyn, too, was well satisfied as she shut the door behind him. It had worked like a charm, shattering for a while his arrogant self-confidence and making him want her more than ever. Now all she had to do was to go out with him while he tried to persuade her to marry him, and then pretend to capitulate when a suitable opportunity arose.

It came, quite by chance, about a week or so later. It was Beric's long lay-over and he had flown out to Bali and back and on his return had taken her out for a meal to Hin's Cookhouse at the top of the Singapore Hilton. After the meal Lyn had excused herself to go to the cloakroom, and on coming out found her way back into the restaurant blocked by a party of male tourists who were waiting for a table. They looked like visiting businessmen who were making the most of being off the leash while living on expenses, and had already all had quite a lot to drink. Lyn went to go round them, but one saw her and attracted the attention of the others.

'Well, whady'a know,' he slurred in a heavy accent.

'A blonde among all these brunettes! A diamond shining in the darkness,' he added in a hazy attempt at being gallant as he put out an arm to stop her.

Another man turned and grinned at her. 'Hallo, honey. Don't go away. You stay and eat with us. Have anything you want,' he offered expansively.

Lyn drew away. 'Please let me pass.' She tried to edge through, but they laughed and blocked her way again.

'Y'see, it's like this,' the first man said as he tried to put his arm round her waist. 'We don't know anyone in Singapore—any girls—and we want to have a good time. Let me explain to you . . .'

'Why not try explaining to me?' Suddenly Beric was there, a look of cold anger in his eyes as he pushed the man away from her, then literally picked him up off his feet and glowered at him.

'It's all right. Really.' Lyn touched his arm and he slowly put the man down again. The tourist took one look at his muscles and disappeared out of Beric's vicinity, fast, his friends close on his heels. 'Let's go, please.'

Lyn, realising that the moment had come, was quiet and withdrawn as they rode back to the hotel. Beric looked at her worriedly, but didn't do more than take her hand. He was still unsure of himself with her, still afraid of pushing her too far and too fast.

At the hotel he went to cross to the lifts, but Lyn hung back. 'No. I—I think I'd like to walk in the garden for a while, if you don't mind.'

'Of course.'

They walked down to the end of the terrace where they could look out over the lights in the harbour, the moon glistening on the water and turning it to molten metal, first silver, then gold. Lyn moved a few feet away and stood alone with her back to him. Her heart was beating very fast with that strange excitement again. She tried to judge the timing just right before she turned to look at him as he stood silently waiting.

'Beric—I . . .' And then she gave a little sob and ran into his arms. 'Hold me! Oh, please hold me.'

'Darling!' There was a note of wonder in his voice as he put his arms round her and held her close.

'Don't let me go. Just hold me—please.' Lyn put her arms round his neck and pressed close against him. Then she lifted her head and said on another sob, 'Oh, Beric, I've been such a fool!' Then she stood on tiptoe to reach up and kiss him.

It was the first time she had ever made the first move or even given herself wholeheartedly in response, and she could feel the shock of it run through his body. His hands tightened convulsively on her waist and then he was kissing her with fierce passion as her mouth opened under his at last.

It was a long time before she was able to speak, and even then Beric went on kissing her eyes, her throat, the curve of her cheek. She tried to draw away, but he wouldn't let her go and she laughed a little. 'Hey, don't you want to hear me say it?'

'Say what?' he murmured against her throat.

Softly she answered, 'That I love you. That I want to marry you.'

His head came up at that and he stared at her, his eyes a flame of light in the darkness. Lyn tried not to let the glow of exultation show in hers—tried to look as if she meant it.

'Oh, my darling girl!' His voice was very soft, full of love and tenderness and an indescribable joy. Gently he put a hand up to either side of her face and gazed into it for a long, long moment before he bent and kissed her mouth almost reverently. Then he smiled at her. 'Perhaps now you'll tell me why you ran away?'

Lyn moved out of his arms and half-turned away. It was so much easier to put on an act when she wasn't looking him straight in the face. 'I did it because I was afraid,' she told him unevenly.

'Of me?'

'No, not entirely.' She hesitated, then went on, 'I was afraid that you'd only asked me to marry you because you knew it was—it was the only way you could have me.'

'But I told you I was in love with you!'

'You might have told yourself that too.'

'Oh, my poor mixed-up darling!' Gently Beric turned her round to face him and she went into his arms again.

'I told you I'd been a fool.'

'Yes, you were.' His arms tightened and for a moment there was anger in his face. 'Don't ever do it again. I went through hell not knowing where you were. If I ever lost you my life wouldn't be worth living.' He held her for a while longer, then said, 'When did you change your mind?'

'Tonight. At the Hilton. I realised that I'd been putting you on a par with those men, the type who's ready to run after anything in skirts, but that you weren't really like that at all. That ever since you made that promise to leave me alone you've kept it and . . .' She broke off suddenly and looked up at him. 'You're laughing at me!'

He laughed aloud at her indignant face. 'Yes, you brainless little idiot. But only just this once. We'll have a whole lifetime when I'll be laughing *with* you instead.'

CHAPTER SIX

THEY were married six weeks later, in the small old parish church near to Beric's home in England. There was, of course, no one of Lyn's there, neither family nor friend, but there were so many of Beric's that they overflowed into her side as well and filled the little church. The crew, too, sat on the bride's side and John Reese, the Flight Engineer, had volunteered to give her away.

It had surprised her at first that he had wanted to be married in church, and she had suggested a registrar's office, but Beric had been adamant, saying that he intended to marry her with all the pomp and ceremony he could contrive. 'From choirboys to bridesmaids,' he told her. 'The whole works.'

Lyn had smiled at him. 'When you fall you really do it in a big way, don't you?'

'With a thud,' he admitted, not in the least rueful, adding, his eyes bright with pride, 'No man could love a woman more than I love you, Netta.'

So she had agreed to the church wedding, had thrown up her job and flown back with him and a stunned crew after his next lay-over. He had wanted her to go and stay with his parents but Lyn had insisted on staying in London so that she could shop for her trousseau. And she had other preparations to make that he wouldn't know about. He was so besotted that it had taken little effort to persuade him to take her to North Africa for their honeymoon and he booked a room at the Tour Khalef Hotel in Sousse in Tunisia.

Once that was settled Lyn was able to get busy. She visited Nadia who was looking after her things for her and collected her old passport in her own name, then she found a well-known travel company who did package holidays to the same hotel and booked a fortnight's holiday in her own name, starting just over a week before the wedding. She then laughingly told Beric that she was putting on weight with all the meals he was buying her and so she was going to go to a health farm for a week before the wedding. He tried to make her change her mind at first, but she insisted, and he eventually gave way when she said she wanted to look her best for him. It didn't take much to make him do what she wanted, he was completely in her power.

On the day she was supposed to go to the health farm, Beric flew out to Singapore for the last time before the wedding; he wouldn't be back until two days before, so there was no fear of him trying to contact her. A few hours later Lyn caught the charter flight to Tunisia and, wearing a brunette wig and without the grey lenses, checked into the Tour Khalef Hotel with the rest of her party as Lynette Maxwell. She went on all the excursions during the first five days, getting to know other people on the package holiday, then casually told the courier that she'd booked to go on a four-day mini-safari trip into the Sahara. Instead she flew back to England and got to London in time to drive out to Heathrow to meet Beric as his plane flew in.

They were together for a few hours in which Lyn didn't have to pretend to be nervous; as the time grew nearer the feelings of anxiety mixed up with extreme excitement became more intense and she felt as if she was living on a knife edge.

The weather was beautiful on the day of the wedding, the sun warm and bright, giving the countryside that mellowness that can only exist in England in early summer. The reception was held out of doors on the lawns of his parents' home, the two bridesmaids—Beric's little nieces—flitting like bright butterflies among the guests. There was the cake to be cut, toasts and speeches, and Beric's eyes, alight with pride and happiness, as he took her hand and spoke of her for the first time as 'my wife'. Then it was time to change and to throw her bouquet to the bunch of elegantly dressed stewardesses and to cheat a little so that Julia caught it. And then they were running in a shower of confetti to a car covered in ribbons and rosettes, with tin cans trailing from the bumper and heavily daubed with 'Just Married' signs.

The crazy excitement was at its height then, but somehow none of it was real. Lyn felt as if she was on a stage playing a part and yet as if she was also watching herself detachedly from the wings, waiting impatiently for the climax of the play. But then Beric's mother, who had been more than kind to her, came to say goodbye.

She kissed Lyn and smiled at her. 'My dear child, welcome to our family. And thank you for making my son so happy.'

That had brought Lyn down to earth with a shock and she had stared at Mrs Dane in consternation until Beric had laughingly put her into the car amid showers of confetti and rose petals, and they had driven away.

A couple of miles down the road Beric stopped to get rid of the ribbons and tin cans, and to wipe away as much of the slogans as he could. Then he spent the next ten minutes thoroughly kissing her, until Lyn breathlessly pushed him away.

'Hey, we don't want to miss the plane.'

'Mm? Just one more. It's a long way to Tunisia.'

'Okay, just one more, but that's all.' She smiled at him. 'We've got all the time in the world.'

They arrived at Sousse in the early evening, driving from the airport along straight, dusty roads, and with Lyn exclaiming with pretended wonder at the sight of women wearing the traditional *sifsari*, a white cloak-cum-shawl, which they wrapped round them to keep off the dirt; the camels in the fields, the flowers and acres of olive trees. Beric smiled at her indulgently and took her hand. She could feel the tension in him which matched her own, but for a very different reason. He had waited a long time for today, for the moment when he would have the right to undress her, to carry her to his bed, to take her body and her virginity. She had held him off for so long that his anticipation now must be at fever pitch, expecting that in just a few hours she would be completely his. Lyn turned her hand in his, smiled at him radiantly and leaned her head on his shoulder. It was something he would remember, something to add to the pain later on.

The hotel was very luxurious, all marble columns and Moorish architecture. They were shown to a room with a balcony facing the gardens and swimming pool, and beyond it the sea. It was very warm, the heat blowing off the Sahara, but it was a dry heat that made a welcome change after the humidity of Singapore.

Beric let Lyn have the bathroom first and she showered, put on clean, delicately lacy underclothes with her bathrobe over them and came out into the bedroom again to put on a dress.

Beric had been sitting on the balcony, smoking a cigarette, but he turned as she came back into the room, ground out the cigarette and came inside.

Lyn hesitated, waited for him to go into the bathroom before she took off the robe, but he came up to her, kissed the back of her neck and then turned her to face him.

'Don't be shy,' he said softly. 'Please, don't ever be shy with me. And don't be afraid. There's nothing to be afraid of.'

For answer she smiled at him tremulously, put her arms round his neck and said softly, 'I'm not afraid. Not any more.'

'Oh, my darling girl!' He kissed her yearningly, his hands at the belt of her robe and then inside. 'Oh, God, Netta, if you only knew how much I want you. It's like a great ache deep inside me. I want to touch you and love you, hold you in my arms and never let you go. Even being apart from you for a few hours is hell; I can think of nothing but being back with you, I never stop longing for you.' He looked down at her, his face tense, his hands tight on her waist, as he strove to describe his emotions. 'Sometimes,' he said slowly, 'I think that my body just isn't big enough to hold all the love I feel for you.'

Lyn stared up at him, bereft of words, but then he kissed her again with ever-increasing passion, pushing the robe from her shoulders so that it fell to the floor. Lyn began to get in a panic in case he wouldn't wait for the night and wanted to make love to her now. And yet she didn't want to have to fight him off, she wanted everything to be sweet and loving between them this evening. That way he would be even more hurt when the time came. So she returned his kisses for a while before gently drawing away.

He groaned and it took some time for him to recover, his heart hammering in his chest, his breathing ragged. 'Sorry.' He grinned ruefully. 'Guess I got carried away.'

He changed and then they went down to the restaurant to eat, and afterwards strolled down towards the pool where all the hotel shops were situated. They looked at the ornate carpets and prayer mats, at the pottery and the leatherwork, then Lyn stopped to admire some filigree silver bracelets.

Turning to Beric, she said hesitatingly, 'I know you gave me those beautiful pearl earrings as a wedding present, but they're very special and not something you could wear all the time. Would you think me terribly greedy if I asked you to buy me one of these bracelets so that I can wear it every day and—and remember being here?'

He did, of course. How could he possibly refuse? And Lyn held the boxed bracelet while they went to sit outside under the trees for a last drink. They didn't hurry and they didn't talk much, just sat and held hands in the warm moonlight. Then Beric stood up abruptly.

'Let's go up, shall we?' His voice was thick and unsteady.

'All right.' Careful not to let him see, Lyn put the box containing the bracelet on to the chair next to hers, under the table. Then she stood up, smiled at him, and let him take her back into the hotel.

They climbed the wide marble stairs and had almost reached their floor when Lyn gave an exclamation of dismay. 'Oh, my bracelet! I must have left it in the garden. Oh, no!' She turned as if to go back, but Beric stopped her.

'It'll be all right. We'll find it in the morning.'

'But someone might steal it.' Lyn looked at him pleadingly, her heart thumping as she put everything into this crucial moment. 'Darling, I'm sorry, but please would you get it for me? I'd hate to lose it.'

'All right.' He grinned. 'Maybe I'll be too pre-occupied in the morning anyway!'

He gave her the key of their room and she bent to kiss him gently on the mouth. 'Hurry back,' she said softly.

He didn't say anything, but his eyes, so intensely blue, told her everything he felt. Then he turned and was running back downstairs.

As soon as he disappeared from sight, Lyn took a hasty look along the corridor, gave an infinite sigh of relief when she saw it was empty, and ran to their room. There she threw open a suitcase that she hadn't yet unpacked, pulled out a large leather handbag that she'd had with her as Lyn Maxwell and with a sweep of her hand pulled other clothes across to fill the gap. From the bag she pulled a long-sleeved dress that she hastily put on over the one she was wearing, then she took the brown wig from the bag and put it on over her own hair. Hands trembling violently, she shut the case, picked up the leather bag, her evening bag and the key, then peeped out to make sure the corridor was still empty. This had been her biggest fear, that someone might be in the corridor and see her enter and leave. But she was lucky again, it was still deserted. Quickly she locked the door behind her and then walked briskly to a door leading to the service stairs farther down the corridor, the whereabouts of which she'd checked on her earlier stay.

Once inside, she leaned against the wall for a moment, trying to control her shaking body, her pounding heartbeats, then she deliberately opened her evening bag and dropped it on the floor, the contents rolling out. The room key she dropped alongside them, then she hurried down the stairs to the ground floor and went into the nearby ladies' cloakroom where she double-checked that the wig was on firmly, and shut herself in a cubicle while she exchanged her elegant high-heeled shoes for a pair of flat sandals that she had ready in the bag. Then she took out the contact lenses and flushed them down the loo, feeling an immense sense of relief that she didn't need to wear them any more.

She waited for a few minutes as she fought to control herself, but she was still feeling almost sick with excitement, the adrenalin bubbling in her veins, when she squared her shoulders and walked out of the ladies', then, as casually as she could manage, strolled into the foyer to go to the reception desk. But she had only taken a few steps when she saw Beric come running down the stairs and she turned in a mad panic and went to gaze blindly at a notice board advertising excursions, her back to the foyer. His voice carried to her quite clearly as he spoke to the man at the reception desk.

'Do you have a pass key for room two-twenty? I need it at once.'

'You have lost your key, monsieur?'

'No, my wife had it.'

'Perhaps, then, if you found your wife . . .'

'You don't understand,' Beric snapped impatiently. 'My wife is already in the room, but she didn't answer when I knocked.'

The receptionist answered delicately, 'In that case, monsieur, your wife may have been on the balcony and not heard you or,' he lowered his voice, 'in the bathroom, perhaps.'

'She would have heard me. She was expecting me.' Beric's voice rose. 'For God's sake hurry up, man! She may be ill.' There was worry and concern in his tone, and Lyn should have heard it with exultation because it was the first sign that her years of thirst for revenge were at last to be satisfied, but strangely she didn't, she could only feel nervous and panicky, her hands gripping each other tightly to stop herself from screaming with tension.

'I will telephone for you,' the man insisted, and picked up the receiver on the desk.

He held on for some minutes and then Beric almost knocked it out of his hand. '*Now* will you get the damn key?' he thundered.

There was no arguing with Beric when he spoke like that and the poor man hastily got the key, called for a colleague to come and take over the desk and went with Beric up the stairs, Beric going up them three at a time and the smaller man running to keep up.

As soon as they were out of sight, Lyn turned, her legs feeling strangely wobbly, and walked over to the desk. 'My key please.'

'Your room number, madam?'

For a mind-freezing moment she couldn't remember the room number she'd had when she first arrived there and almost blurted out two-twenty, the room she was supposed to be sharing with Beric, but then, thank goodness, it came back.

'Three-three-six,' she said in a strangled voice.

The man handed over the key and she moved to the stairs. It was the longest, hardest climb she had ever made in her life. As she passed the second floor she caught a glimpse of Beric and the receptionist. They were standing by the open door and obviously arguing, but it was too far away for Lyn to hear what was being said. She went up to the next floor, along the corridor to her old room, and literally collapsed on the bed, her legs no longer able to support her, feeling completely drained of energy and strength.

She lay there for hours, imagining what was happening, seeing Beric searching everywhere for her and growing ever more frantic with worry as the time passed. And with frustration too, she thought, smiling grimly in the darkened room; he would be spending his wedding night in a far different way from what he had hoped and waited so long for. What sort of assistance was he getting from the hotel staff? she wondered. Very little, probably. They must be used to couples having rows on holiday and one or other of them going off. No, they probably wouldn't even take him very seriously until her bag was found, which would only increase Beric's fury and frustration, and it was quite possible for the bag not to be found until the maids came in in the morning. So that Beric would go through a night of hell wondering where she was.

A wave of nausea suddenly filled her and she got up and went into the bathroom. She gripped the edge of the basin and tried to fight off the feeling, stood there until it went away. She felt curiously flat and deflated, completely empty of emotion, rather how she thought a drug addict must feel after the effects of the last fix had worn off. Slowly she got undressed and ready for bed, carefully folding up the blue dress she had been

wearing when she was with Beric and locking it away
in her case; tomorrow she would have to get rid of
that, just in case all the rooms in the hotel were
searched. She looked at the dainty underwear and
began to tremble again; he'd seen that, too, touched it,
and had almost lost control. Lyn suddenly picked up
the wispy pieces of silk and began to tear viciously at
the lace, then stopped abruptly, heart pounding. What
the hell was she doing?

Grimly she put them away and got into bed, her
imagination still working overtime and much too
wound up to sleep. A short time later she heard the
whine of a police siren that stopped outside the hotel.
Either they had found her bag or Beric had used the
force of his personality and insisted they be called. Lyn
lay awake all night, listening. Many of the noises earlier
on were probably those of guests returning from the
night-club or evening excursions, but there were other
sounds, too; more police cars, booted feet walking
along the corridor, and voices issuing commands outside.

As soon as it was light, Lyn got up and looked out
of the window. A row of policemen were systematically
searching the gardens, and she could just make out
some more men down on the beach, and a boat with
what looked like a couple of divers in it a short way
out from the shore. The sight startled her; it hadn't
occurred to her that they might think she'd committed
suicide.

That day she had booked to go on an excursion to
Monastir, so she had an early breakfast and waited in
the foyer with other people from her tour for the coach.
There was a great deal of coming and going; a uni-
formed policeman was on duty by the door and it

looked as if some others in plain clothes had taken over a small office behind the reception desk and were interviewing some members of the staff. Lyn recognised one of the waiters who had served them last night and her heart skipped a beat. The guests around her were all chattering excitedly, wondering what it was all about and making rash surmises.

The coach came and they all stood up and tramped outside into the hot sun. Lyn, like everyone else, put on sunglasses to cut down the glare, and got into the coach, sitting alone by a window. As she waited for the coach to fill, a car drew up and three men got out. One of them was Beric. He was still dressed in the clothes he had had on last night, and as he turned for a moment to speak to one of the other men she caught a glimpse of his face. In that instant she knew that her revenge was complete. His face was drawn and haggard, his mouth set into a hard, tight line of scarcely controlled anguish. And his eyes, usually such a vivid blue, were dark with agonising pain and torment. He looked like a man who had been held down and beaten into the ground.

At Monastir everyone paid their hundred millimes and trailed round the ancient Ribat of Harthema, and the younger people climbed the eighty-seven steps to the top of the watch-tower to admire the view of the town and the coast. There was a break then for lunch and most of the people disappeared towards the souvenir shops, but Lyn went down to the beach and hired a pedalo, taking it far over to one side of the bay and far enough out to where she thought the gently shelving bottom was as deep as she could reasonably dive down to. There, where no one could see her, she took off the wig and replaced it with a bathing cap, then

unwound the blue dress from where she had hidden it
in her beach towel and dived down with it to bury it in
a hole she dug out of the sea bottom, covering it with
sand and small rocks so that there was no chance of it
floating up again. It took several dives and she felt
exhausted when she had finished, but she at least felt
confident that it would never be found and glad that it
was done. It would have been the end of everything if
it had been discovered in her room.

She didn't see Beric again that day or the next, but
by then it was all round the hotel that a woman had
been kidnapped, and she had a shock when a policeman
stopped her, and everyone else, when they left the
dining-room and showed them a copy of her passport
photograph.

'Pardon, madame,' the policeman said, 'but we are
looking for this woman who arrived at the hotel two
days ago. Have you seen her?'

Somehow Lyn managed to shake her head. 'No. No,
I haven't.'

Most of the rest of the day she spent in the Medina,
the old walled town with its Minotaur's maze of narrow
streets and cul-de-sacs, each named after the type of
wares sold in the street: the Souk des Etoffes was the
cloth market, then there was the wool market, the per-
fume market, the gold market—the list seemed end-
less. But Lyn walked with a purpose, because she
hadn't finished with Beric yet. The knife had to be
turned in the wound quite a lot more before she was
through.

She found what she was looking for near the silk
market; here there were four ways which met near a
small fountain, and just a few feet down one of the
roads there was a flight of stone stairs, almost hidden

behind one of the stalls, which twisted up in the thickness of the wall to a rebuilt palace that tourists could go round, this being a secondary entrance that few people used, marked only with a chipped and dirty signboard.

That evening and all the next day the hotel was invaded by reporters and cameramen, and when Lyn bought a day-old English newspaper she found one of the wedding photographs of herself and Beric on the front page under the headline 'BRIDE DISAPPEARS ON WEDDING DAY', and under it, 'Englishwoman feared kidnapped'. It seemed so strange to see it written down in black and white, it suddenly made the play become real, and Lyn hastily screwed up the newspaper and threw it away.

There was a cabaret at the night-club in the grounds of the hotel that evening and Lyn went along to watch. She stayed until about three in the morning and then evaded the little Arabian boys who waited outside to sell bunches of jasmine and walked down into the town until she found a telephone booth near the Medina. Then she dialled the number of the Tour Khalef, and when they answered spoke in French, pretending to be the operator. 'You're through to the Hotel Tour Khalef.'

'Th-thank you.' In her own voice, but making it sound slurred and uneven, she asked for room two-twenty.

'Please—I have to speak to Mr Dane.' She made it sound urgent, and the next moment she heard the phone ring.

'Hello?' It was Beric's voice. He answered it instantly, as if he'd been near the phone. His voice was raw and sharp, but he sounded deathly tired. She wondered how long he had been sitting by the phone, waiting for news, waiting for a ransom demand, perhaps.

He said hello again before Lyn said, 'Beric?' on a low, gasping sob.

'Netta! Oh, dear God! Darling, where are you? What happened to you?' His voice was a crazy mixture of thankfulness, hope and anxiety.

'Oh, Beric!' She tried to sound as if she was crying, but then she heard another click on the line and realised that someone else was listening in. They would be trying to trace the call in case she'd really been kidnapped. She would have to hurry.

Beric said again urgently, 'Netta, where are you?'

'I—I'm not sure. They made me drink something and—and I felt so strange and I couldn't see properly. But I think—I think I'm somewhere in the market. We came—we came past a fountain. But I . . .'

His voice rough with anxiety, Beric broke in, 'Netta, the phone. Look at the number on it. Tell me what it is.'

'I can't. It's dark, and I don't know how to light the lamp. They tied me to the bed, but I got free. Oh, Beric,' her voice rose on a sob, 'please help me! They're going to take me away tomorrow morning, I heard them say so. I . . . Oh, no! He's coming back. Oh, God no!' She screamed into the mouthpiece. 'No, please!' and dropped the receiver with a crash.

She heard Beric shouting her name in a frenzy of despair, then she deliberately picked up the receiver and cut off his voice.

She walked back to the hotel along the beach, wading in the shallows, confident that there hadn't been time to trace the call. As she walked along under the stars it came to her that what she had done was pure sadism.

But then she remembered the three years she had spent in prison and her mouth set into a bitter line. Sadism or not, there was no way she was going to stop now until the wound she had dealt him was as mortal as she could possibly make it!

The next morning she went quite openly back to the Medina, sharing a taxi with several other people who were doing some last-minute shopping. Adroitly she avoided the tentacles of a couple who liked to collect people and who wanted her and the others to walk around in a group, and made her way along to the silk market, not hurrying and keeping her eyes open. As she'd guessed, they had picked up her tip about the fountain and there were several men hanging around who could be policemen in plain clothes. She strolled past, secure in her disguise, and was part way up the street of the leatherworkers before she saw Beric. He was standing in the shade of a stall just a few yards up the street. There were two other men with him and they looked as if they were having difficulty in stopping him from pulling the place apart in search of her. Lyn edged into a group of tourists who were passing and went back into the silk market near the staircase.

For a while she stood unobtrusively near the back of a stall, pretending to examine some silks, her heart thundering in her chest again, but feeling strangely calm as she waited for the right moment. Two Arab men dressed in loose black robes came out of a nearby alleyway. Keeping herself hidden by the hanging silks, Lyn quickly pulled off the wig and glasses and darted out to cannon into the two men, who automatically reached out to stop her. Then she screamed out over the top of the noise of the market, 'Help me! Beric, help me!' and dived back between the stalls and up to

the hidden staircase before the two men could gather
their wits. Hastily Lyn ran up the stairs, stuffing her
hair back under the wig. Even if Beric hadn't seen
her, either he or one of the policemen would certainly
have heard her and already be searching the area. Perhaps the two men would hold them up for a while if
they stopped to question them, but there was still a
risk.

But somehow the element of risk and danger helped,
added to the excitement, to the wild, crazy pounding
of her heart. Inside the palace she slipped unobtrusively
into a group of holidaymakers who were being given a
guided tour and checked her reflection in the glass of a
picture to make sure the wig was on straight.

There was the sound of a commotion down below in
the street and Lyn and several others crossed to the
windows to look out. She found she was looking down
into the silk market. One of the unfortunate Arabs she
had chosen for her charade was lying on the ground,
apparently unconscious, and about five policemen were
holding on to Beric's arms, trying to forcibly restrain
him from knocking down the other. Lyn stood looking
down at the desperation in his face for a long moment,
then she turned on her heel and walked briskly away.
The next day she returned to England with the other
members of the package holiday.

CHAPTER SEVEN

'BRITISH AIRWAYS regret to announce that there will be a further delay of one hour on Flight 907 to London.'

The voice over the tannoy repeated the announcement in French and the passengers squeezed into the departure lounge at Nice airport groaned collectively; this was the third delay and the flight was already an hour and a half overdue.

Lyn settled back in her seat with a sigh and picked up the fashion magazine that she'd looked through twice already. She glanced at her watch: six o'clock. Even if the plane did take off at seven, she still wouldn't get home to her London flat until late in the evening. But thank goodness it was Saturday tomorrow and she would be able to have a long sleep and a thoroughly lazy day. The last two weeks had been absolutely hectic; as part of her job in the public relations department of a big industrial and electronics company, she had had to escort three lots of potential customers round their French branches, acting as interpreter and making sure they were properly accommodated and entertained, and on top of that had also sandwiched in a flying visit to Basle to check on the arrangements for the company's stand at an international trade fair which opened next month. She enjoyed the job she had got shortly after returning to England from Tunisia, and found it a constant challenge, but after nearly fifteen months it had become more than a little exhausting. And now, owing to some technical fault, all British Airways DC 10s had been grounded for tests, and there was this long delay.

There was always the possibility, of course, of switching to another airline, but when she made enquiries Lyn was told that the only available seats were on an Air International flight which was stopping at Nice to refuel on the way back to London from South Africa. This she had hastily rejected; better to wait than run even the slightest risk of running into anyone she might have known in the airline. She might not even be recognised now that her hair was back to its natural colour, but there was always the risk. No, so long as she kept away from Air International she would be safe.

After half an hour or so she got up and went to the ladies' to freshen up and then had to hurriedly dry her hands and rush out when the tannoy announced that a replacement aircraft had been found for Flight 907 which was being boarded at once at Gate Eleven. It was all a bit chaotic, no one having reserved seat numbers and the smokers trying to push down to the back and vice versa. Lyn found an empty seat in the non-smoking section next to an elderly woman and sat down out of the way. She would rather have sat by the window, but it couldn't be helped. The last of the passengers got themselves settled, the doors were closed and the plane began to taxi towards the runway as the stewardess came round to check that all the safety belts were fastened. Lyn glanced up and froze with shock. The stewardess was wearing the all too familiar uniform of Air International!

As the girl went by Lyn reached out and stopped her. 'I—I thought this was supposed to be a British

Airways flight?' she managed hoarsely.

'Yes, madam, it is.'

'But that isn't a British Airways uniform.'

The girl smiled. 'No, that's right. It's Air International. You see, this whole plane, plus the crew, is on hire to British Airways until the DCs are back in service again.'

'Oh, I—I see. Thank you.' Lyn sat back in her seat, trying to tell herself to stop panicking, that Air International had hundreds of planes and the chances of seeing anyone she knew were remote. But when the other stewardess brought the drinks round and Lyn saw that she was a complete stranger, she was so relieved that she bought herself two gin and tonics instead of one. She drank one down quickly and leaned back in the seat. She'd needed that! For a while she had got so panicky that she'd even contemplated doing something crazy like demanding to be let off the plane. And what a fool that would have made her look!

Lyn leaned the seat back and tried to sleep as the plane droned on through the sky, the flaming colours of the September sunset reflecting on the silver wings. But her nerves were strung up now and she couldn't sleep. She moved restlessly, disturbing the silk scarf that she'd tied gypsy-fashion over her hair. She tried to straighten it, but it was awkward without a mirror so she decided to go down to the loo in the tail of the plane. Picking up her bag, she made her way down the gangway. Most of the passengers were reading or trying to sleep, and the plane was quiet. Both of the loos were occupied and she had to stand outside and wait. The two stewardesses who served the rear end of the plane were working in the curtained-off galley

section, but then a call button buzzed and one came
out to answer it.

'Netta!'

Before Lyn had a chance to turn her back or even
look away she'd been recognised—by Julia Connors,
the girl in Beric's crew that she'd used to get to know
him. Her mind went numb and she could only stand
there, as transfixed with shock as the other girl. Then
the door of one of the lavatories opened as someone
came out and Lyn dived into it like a rabbit going into
a hole. As she shut the door she caught a glimpse of
Julia starting to hurry up the gangway towards the
front of the plane.

Safely inside, Lyn leaned against the door, the slight
continuous vibration of the plane lost beneath the
shaking of her own body. Of all the infernal luck, that
Julia should be on this plane and had come out of the
galley at that precise moment! Now her only hope was
to brazen it out and make Julia think she'd been mistaken. After all, Lyn Maxwell really didn't look a lot
like the late lamented Netta Dane, née Lewis. But then
Lyn looked in the mirror and gave a groan. Oh, what a
fool! With the scarf tied over her hair, covering it, the
only thing that had been different was the colour of
her eyes. Julia had been bound to recognise her!

Well, at least she could remedy that straightaway.
Hastily she took out the clips holding her hair up and
let it fall long and loose down to her shoulders, then
took out a brush to tidy it and pull it forward over her
forehead as much as she could. She had hardly finished
when she heard someone outside and then a man's
voice said imperatively, 'Which one?' and Lyn's heart
froze in mind-bending fear. So that was why Julia had
gone hurrying up the gangway. To fetch Beric. He

must be flying the damn plane!

Lyn stood and stared at her chalk-white reflection in the mirror, trying to force her mind to work, trying agonisingly to think of some way out. If there had been a way of walking through the fabric of the plane she would have done it, anything rather than face him. Somehow she managed to pull herself together a little and realised that her only hope was in convincing them that they'd made a mistake. But then Beric would demand to look at her passport and he'd see her name. Unless—unless she could take the wind out of his sails first.

Quickly she reached inside her bag again, but as she did so an imperative knock sounded on the door and she nearly dropped the whole lot.

'J-just a minute,' she managed to call, while feverishly pulling out some eyeshadow and putting it on her lids, and then adding mascara and a bright red lipstick. As Netta Lewis she had always worn very soft make-up, so even this pathetic attempt at disguise might help. She flushed the loo, ran some water in the basin while she crammed the make-up back in her bag, then took a deep breath to vainly try and control the thundering of her heart, and opened the door.

She stepped out, said, 'Sorry to keep you waiting,' without looking up and went to step past them.

Beric's hand shot out and gripped her arm so tightly that she almost cried out. 'Just a moment.' His voice was tense and rasping, as if he could hardly trust himself to speak.

It took every ounce of courage Lyn could summon to make herself turn round and raise her eyes to look at him. The shock was total! This wasn't the same man she had left behind in Tunisia. The same basic facial features, yes, but this man had lines of pain and grief etched into his face, his eyes were hard and guarded, and, where once his mouth had curled in cynicism, it now twisted with bitterness and continuous torment. His eyes widened in surprise as he stared at her, for the moment uncertain.

Lyn somehow let recognition come into her own face and then she smiled at him, praying that he wouldn't notice what a travesty she had made of it.

'Why, Beric! What a surprise!' The grip on her arm tightened convulsively and she added hastily. 'I am right, aren't I? You are Beric Dane?'

'Yes,' he bit out curtly, the blue eyes watching her narrowly, like a hawk about to pounce.

Lyn tried to laugh lightly, but even to her own ears it sounded strangled and false. 'It's been such a long time I hardly recognised you.' She looked up at him again. 'Look, you do know who I am, don't you?' Adding, as she nodded towards where he was holding her, 'Otherwise why did you stop me?'

Beric was still staring at her, his eyes glittering. 'I'm afraid your name escapes me for a moment.'

'It's Lyn. Lyn Maxwell. We—flew together for a while some years ago.'

To her intense relief she saw a stunned, stupefied look come into his eyes and the grip on her arm relaxed, although he didn't let go entirely. Slowly he said, 'I'm sorry. I didn't recognise you.'

'Oh. That wasn't why you stopped me, then?'

'No. The stewardess thought you were someone else.'

Julia chimed in, 'But, Beric, I could have sworn that . . .'

'No!' Beric cut her off curtly. 'You were mistaken.' He made a dismissive gesture with his hand and Julia reluctantly moved away. Then he turned back to Lyn. 'It's strange, I somehow remember you differently.'

She laughed again, more easily this time. 'I am different. People change in—what must it be?—nearly five years. I was a lot plumper then, anyway.'

'Yes.' His eyes ran over her, and Lyn suddenly felt as if she was standing there completely naked. Her hands automatically moved to cover herself, but then she hastily stopped, hoping he hadn't noticed.

'Well,' she gave a forced smile, 'I mustn't keep you from flying the plane. Nice seeing you again.'

He nodded, and Lyn turned to walk up the gangway, but she could feel his eyes boring into her back all the way to her seat.

She managed to avoid looking at him as he went back to the cockpit, and then she could only sit in her seat, gripping the arms and praying for the journey to end. 'Oh please, God, get me off this plane. Please, please, get me off this plane!'

At last it came in to land, but so smoothly that she could hardly feel it as the giant aircraft tires brushed the concrete runway and then the reverse thrust brought them to a sedate speed. If meeting her had thrown Beric it certainly didn't show in the way he handled the plane.

Lyn was one of the first people to disembark, hurrying along the echoing corridors, too impatient to take the moving pavement, intent on putting as much space between herself and the plane as possible, and of course reaching the baggage reception point ages before the first of the luggage arrived. For a few moments she contemplated not bothering to claim her cases, to just walk out and come back for them some other time. But that would look suspicious, as if she was trying to avoid

taking them through Customs, and with her record
they would go through her things meticulously. No,
better to wait and go through as normal.

After what seemed an agonisingly long time, she
managed to retrieve both her cases and put them on a
trolley. She went through the 'Nothing to Declare'
section and wasn't even stopped. Then she was out in
the main body of the airport and hurrying towards the
exit doors and the waiting taxi rank.

'That looks heavy. Why don't you let me push it for
you?'

For the third time that night Lyn's heart froze with
shock as Beric appeared from nowhere and forcefully
took the trolley from her resistless grasp.

'Oh, but I . . .'

'Where are you heading?' he asked her, then looked
quite openly at the labels on her luggage. 'I see you
live in Swiss Cottage?'

'Yes.'

'Do you have a car here?'

'No. I'm going to get a train,' she lied, hoping he'd
go away.

'This is your lucky day, then,' he told her. 'I'm going
that way myself, and I can drop you off.'

'That really isn't necessary.' Lyn tried to protest,
thinking that this was turning out to be one of the
*un*luckiest days of her life.

'Nonsense. I expect you're tired after that long wait
at Nice. You surely don't *want* to go on the train?' He
turned and looked at her as he spoke, suspicion in his
voice and his eyes.

Lyn knew immediate, nightmarish fear. 'No, of
course not. If—if you're sure it isn't taking you out of
your way?'

'Not at all.' To her relief the suspicion faded and he pushed the trolley through the doors and turned in the direction of the aircrew's car park.

As she walked along beside him, hurrying a little to keep up with his long strides, it occurred to Lyn that the crews didn't usually come this way round, they could go through a different way to the car park. So what did that mean? That it hadn't been a coincidence that Beric was leaving the terminal building at the same time? That he'd deliberately waylaid her? Fear gripped her again and her steps faltered.

But Beric, too, had stopped. 'Here we are.'

He took some keys from his pocket and unlocked the trunk of an expensive-looking silver Aston Martin. Lyn wondered whether he'd paid for it out of his salary, or out of the money he'd got from trafficking in drugs. And suddenly she wasn't afraid any more, the old anger and hate that she hadn't felt for a long time now coming back and filling her heart and mind.

Beric glanced up from stowing her cases in the boot and became still, his eyes fixed on her face. Lyn smiled at him coolly, for the first time that night having her emotions under control. Slowly Beric straightened up and shut the trunk. 'Let's go, shall we?' he said without looking at her again.

He drove the silver car smoothly through the traffic, taking advantage of its powerful engine to overtake whenever a gap appeared so that they were soon through the old City of London, the very heart of England, dominated by St Paul's Cathedral and the tall spires of all the old churches rebuilt after the Great Fire. He hardly spoke at all, only once to ask her to open up a carton of duty-free cigarettes on the parcel shelf and hand him a packet. The packet he opened expertly with one hand, lighting the cigarette he took from it with the dashboard lighter.

'Sorry.' He offered the pack to Lyn. 'Do you smoke now? I know you didn't used to before.'

'No.' Lyn shook her head. 'I never have.' And wondered, if he remembered that, how much more he would remember about her. The shape of her nose, for instance. Her hands gripped the bag in her lap until the knuckles showed white.

He cut through Regent's Park, heading north now, then pulled into the car park at the side of a pub.

'Let's go in and have a drink.'

'Thanks,' Lyn's voice was curt, 'but I'd rather get home, if you don't mind.'

Beric turned to look at her and suddenly the car seemed filled with menace. But his tone was quite bland as he said, 'Ten minutes won't make any difference, surely? Not after the delay you've had already.'

Lyn bit her lip, hating the thought of having to sit and drink with him, and yet afraid of arousing his suspicions if she refused. Reluctantly she answered, 'All right, but just one. I'm really very tired.'

'Of course.'

He came round to open the door for her and Lyn carefully avoided touching him as she got out.

The pub was one of those oases of comfort and tradition that can still be found tucked away down little side streets even in the centre of London. The ceiling was low-beamed so that Beric had to duck his head, and dim lighting revealed little tables in odd corners. A log fire burned in an inglenook fireplace, taking the chill out of the evening air, the flames reflected in the burnished glow of dozens of copper jugs, horse brasses, and pewter mugs that lined the walls and hung from the beams.

Lyn sat down at one of the tables while Beric went to the bar to get the drinks. He stood with his back towards her, the material of his uniform jacket stretched taut across his broad shoulders, and Lyn found that her throat had gone dry and her heart had started to beat in that crazy way it used to when she was with him before. She tried to look away, but somehow her eyes kept coming back to him.

He brought the drinks and raised his glass to her. 'Cheers. What were you doing in France?' he asked her after he'd taken a drink. 'On holiday?'

'Yes, that's right,' Lyn lied. 'I was there for two weeks.'

His left eyebrow rose. 'Alone?'

Lyn's chin came up defiantly. 'Yes.'

His eyes narrowed for a moment, but he didn't pursue it. 'What work do you do now? I take it you're not in flying any more?'

'No,' Lyn agreed coldly, 'I'm not in flying any more.' For a moment their eyes met and held, then she looked down at her glass as she played with the stem. 'I do clerical work,' she said abruptly. 'Typing, filing, that kind of thing.'

'In London?'

'Yes.'. She forced herself to look at him. 'And you?' She nodded at the four gold rings on his sleeve. 'I see you're a fully-fledged captain now. But I thought you preferred the long-range flights rather than short hauls to and from France?'

'Yes, I used to do all long range flying, but I changed over quite recently so that I could spend more time in Europe.' He picked up his glass to drink, but his eyes watched her as he did so; he had hardly taken his eyes off her for a second ever since he had sat down.

Lyn sat back in her seat, trying not to let him see how tense she was. She glanced at her watch. 'They'll be closing soon, won't they?'

'Not for a while yet; they stay open later on Friday nights.' He eyed her contemplatively. 'No one's expecting you, are they? You haven't got anyone waiting for you?' Deliberately he reached out and took hold of her left wrist, lifted it so that her hand was on the table. 'I see that you're not married or engaged.'

'No.' Lyn pressed her hand hard against the table top, kept it rigid to try and stop it from shaking, praying that he wouldn't feel it. 'No, I'm not.'

'And there's no one—special?'

'No.' The word was short and cold. She snatched her hand away and put it back safely under the table.

A silence fell between them, but it seemed to Lyn as if he was waiting, expecting her to say something. And suddenly, with a sick feeling in her chest, she realised what it was. If she was the innocent person she was pretending to be, there was only one thing to say now. She bit her lip and not looking at him directly, said awkwardly, 'I—I'm sorry about your wife. I read about it in the papers.'

Something flickered in his eyes, then his lids came down, shutting the world out from his pain. 'Yes.'

'Did she ... Was she ever ...?' Lyn floundered, wishing she was anywhere but in this chair, facing this man.

'No,' Beric said abruptly, reaching for his drink again. 'No trace of her was ever found.' He took a long swallow, then leant back in his seat, openly studying her face. 'As a matter of fact you look a lot like she did. Different colour eyes and hair, of course, but otherwise very similar. In fact the stewardess on the plane thought that you *were* Netta. My wife,' he added in explanation.

'Oh!' Lyn let her eyes open wide in surprise. 'That's right, I remember now she did call me that, but I didn't take much notice at the time. So *that's* why you were waiting to grab me?' She raised her eyebrows and gave a short laugh. 'And I thought it was because you'd remembered me from all those years ago.'

'I'm afraid not.' Beric kept his eyes fixed on her face. 'But the likeness is really amazing.'

Lyn laughed again. 'Oh, I don't find it all that surprising, really. Don't all men go for a type? They subconsciously decide on what suits them and always pick out girls with the same sort of face and figure. Why, I bet lots of your girl-friends have looked like me,' she added, desperately trying to sidetrack him.

'Possibly.' Beric bent to light another cigarette. 'You seem to have become quite an expert on men,' he said as he blew out the smoke, his eyes narrowed against it.

'Hardly,' Lyn snapped. His eyebrows rose disbelievingly, so she added bitingly, 'You don't get a great deal of opportunity to meet men in a women's prison!'

There was a sudden sharp silence, and Lyn wished she could curl up and die. Why the hell had she said that? She hadn't meant it at all. It had just slipped out, full of the old bitterness.

'But that was all over long ago,' Beric remarked blandly. 'How long did you get—a year?'

'Three years.' God, he'd cared so little that he couldn't even remember how long they'd shut her away for.

He drew on his cigarette. 'But surely you weren't in

there for all that long? There must have been remission
for good behaviour, and parole, that sort of thing?'

'No. I was in Holloway for the whole three years.'
Picking up her glass, Lyn drained it down and then
stood up, careful not to let her feelings show. 'If you
don't mind, I'd like to get home.'

'Of course.' Beric finished his drink and got to his
feet. He hadn't said anything and his expression hadn't
altered, but as Lyn preceded him out to the car, she
had the uncanny feeling that somehow he knew exactly
what she was thinking.

They drove on to her flat without incident, Lyn
directing him once they had left the main road. She
would have liked to have given him false directions,
but to have done so would have been abysmally
stupid; he had read the labels on her cases and she had
no doubt that he would realise it if she tried to trick him.
When they drew up outside her building, Lyn went to get
out, but he stopped her.

'Look, one of the other pilots is throwing a surprise
party tomorrow to celebrate his wife's birthday at a
holiday cottage down in Kent. Quite a few people from
the airline are going and I wondered whether you'd
like to come along.'

'Thanks,' Lyn retorted shortly, 'but I have quite a
lot to catch up on tomorrow.'

'Okay, then I'll come round in the evening instead
and take you out to dinner.'

'No . . .' Lyn began, but Beric had reached out to
cup her chin. His fingers scorched through her skin
and she jumped as if she'd been burnt.

He smiled and said persuasively, 'We had something
going for us once, Lyn, before that silly misunderstanding. Maybe we could find it again.'

Lyn stared at him. A silly misunderstanding! Was that how he described two people accusing each other of one of the worst crimes you could possibly commit? Her voice grating, she said fiercely, 'I don't go out with married men.'

He laughed harshly then, the ugliness of the sound making Lyn go cold. 'Married? When my wife disappeared on our wedding day? That was over a year ago, Lyn. And all I'm asking you to do is to either have dinner or go to a party with a whole crowd of other people.' His hand tightened for a moment, then he took it away. 'Now that I've met you again, I'd like to keep in touch. I'm in England most of the time and we could see each other often.'

The chill seemed to grow and fill every part of Lyn's body. Her mind, too, seemed frozen, but she tried to force herself to think. She could tell him that she didn't want to see him again, but guessed that he wouldn't take no for an answer, and besides, in her first terror, she had been too friendly back on the plane. He knew where she lived, would keep coming after her until he wore her down. No, she had to have time to run again, to get out of her flat and move into a hotel so that he couldn't find her. So maybe it would be better to pretend to go along with him.

'This party tomorrow,' she said at length. 'What time would we have to leave to go to it?'

'Oh, not until about seven in the evening. It only takes just over an hour to drive down there.'

'That should give me time to get all my chores done. All right, I'll come to the party with you. It might be fun.'

'It will be. Rob Freeman—that's the other pilot—always gives great parties.' He got her bags out of the trunk and carried them up to her flat for her, then raised his hand in farewell., 'See you tomorrow, then. I'll pick you up at seven.'

Which, Lyn thought as she thankfully closed the door, would give her ample time to get some sleep before she packed up and moved out, this time somewhere so far away that there would never be another chance of running into Beric again.

But although she was so tired, she didn't sleep much that night; her mind was too full of Beric, of the way he had looked, the lines in his face that seemed to have made him age ten years instead of one. And her body was so restless and hot even though the night wasn't too warm and the windows were open. At six she got up, made herself some breakfast and then grimly began to pack. It was unfortunate that it was a Saturday as it was extremely unlikely that she'd be able to find somewhere that would take her stuff and store it until she found a new place to live. She would just have to take the chance and come back to the flat some other time, or better still arrange for it to be collected.

At eight-thirty she phoned for a taxi to pick her up at nine, too tense and nervous to do the packing properly and the flat becoming more claustrophobic by the minute so that she felt that she just had to get away. Five minutes later the bell rang. Darn! The cab company must have got her message wrong and sent a taxi straightaway. But it didn't really matter, she would be glad to get out of the place. Slipping a jacket over her blouse and pleated linen skirt, Lyn went to open the door.

She supposed she ought to have known that the fates were against her, but it still came as a shock when she opened the door and found Beric leaning nonchalantly

against the wall. He was dressed casually in tan
trousers, a cotton shirt and lightweight cream sweater.
He smiled at her, and walked into the flat before she
had time to recover from the shock.

He looked round at the packed cases, the hastily tied
bundles of books and the overflowing cardboard boxes,
then turned to look at her, a hard bright glint in his
blue eyes. 'Going somewhere, Lyn?' he asked with
menacing softness.

'What?' Somehow she managed to pull herself together, to shut the door and turn round to face him.
'Oh, no. I just didn't bother to unpack last night.'

He gestured towards the boxes. 'You've only just
moved in here?'

Lyn was about to say yes, but realised that if he was
suspicious he could quite easily check with the caretaker, so she shook her head. 'No. Those things belong to a friend. She was living with a man, but they
had a row and she came to stay here while I was
away—on holiday.'

'She's here now?'

Lyn gave a little sigh of relief, grateful that he'd
accepted the lie. 'No, she's gone home for the week-
end.' Adding, with a flash of brilliance, 'She left a note
saying she'd be sending for her stuff on Monday.' She
looked at him standing in the middle of the room,
making it shrink, turning it from the safe haven she
had made for herself into a place she had to run from,
and resentment for a moment replaced the wild, fearful
beating of her heart. 'You're just slightly early, aren't
you?' she said sarcastically. 'We said seven this evening.'

'I know. Sorry.' Beric smiled at her ruefully. 'I'm
afraid there's been a change of plan. The chap who

was going to get the place ready for the party has let Rob down. He can't make it until this afternoon. So Rob asked me if I'd go down this morning and let the caterers in, make sure there's enough booze, hang the coloured lanterns, that kind of thing.'

'I see. You want me to meet you there, then?' Lyn asked, trying to keep the raw relief from showing in her voice.

'Why, no. I thought we could drive down this morning, spend the day together.'

'I'm sorry,' she answered shortly, 'but I told you I've got too much to do today.'

'Surely you could leave it until tomorrow?'

'No, I have to shop and go to the launderette and . . .'

Deliberately Beric moved towards her and put his hands on her shoulders. Lyn's voice trailed off and she dug her nails hard into her palms to stop herself trembling. Bending his head, he gently brushed her lips with his, hardly touching them, and yet making her pulses start to race and her heart jump crazily. 'You do want to go with me, don't you?' he said softly.

'Yes. Yes, of course I do,' Lyn tried to say it with conviction, 'but I'd much rather join you there this evening.'

'It's off the beaten track. You'd need a car.'

'So I'll hire one.'

'I can't let you do that. Besides, you'll never be able to find the place on your own. Much easier to come with me now.'

He was going to add something else, but just then the doorbell rang again, and as he was standing nearest Beric turned to open it.

The man standing there said all too clearly, 'You

ordered a taxi to the Queen's Palace Hotel.'

Beric stiffened and shot Lyn a quick, knife-edged glance, then he took some money from his pocket and gave it to the cab-driver. 'Thanks, but we won't be needing it now.' Deliberately, then, he shut the door and turned to look at her, his eyebrows raised quizzically. 'The Queen's Palace Hotel?'

But Lyn had had a precious few seconds in which to think. 'It's right next door to my hairdresser's. I wanted to have it done before the party.'

'Your hair looks fine to me.'

He stood and looked at her steadily, and Lyn suddenly knew that there was no way she was going to get out of going with him. He'd made up his mind and she would just have to go along with it, try to go on bluffing it out. To refuse or to protest any further would only arouse his suspicions again. She shrugged. 'All right, I'll come down with you now.' Crossing to one of her cases, she opened it and took out an Indian cotton dress. 'Will I be able to change there?'

'Of course. And you might as well bring a swimsuit; the day's turning really warm and we'll be able to swim and sunbathe this afternoon.'

Lyn found a one-piece suit and packed it with the dress and some toiletries in her leather totebag.

'Ready?' he asked.

She had never felt less ready in her life, but somehow she managed to smile at him. 'Yes, quite ready.'

'Good.' He took her bag from her and put an arm round her waist as he ushered her towards the door. 'I promise you we'll have a day to remember.'

As Beric had said, the day was turning very warm,

the weather apparently settling in to one of those long, hot spells, a last burst of full-blown summer before the leaves started to change colour for autumn. Ordinarily Lyn would have enjoyed the drive down into Kent, the garden of England, but her thoughts were too full of the man beside her, her mind a jumble of past memories, of future fears. She tried to work out his motives for taking her out: was it just because she was an old flame and he thought it might be worth picking up where they left off? Or was it because she reminded him of his wife? She was pretty sure that his first suspicions were completely allayed, but there was always the risk that she might make a slip, and she grew cold with fear at the thought of what he might do to her if he ever found out the truth. Dear God, just let her get through today so that she could get away from him!

Then it suddenly occurred to her that he might have other ideas, that he might want to go to bed with her that night, and her heart jerked in her chest. She sneaked a quick glance at his profile as he guided the car through the traffic heading for the coast. His face looked stern and hard, his mouth set into a thin line, a slight frown of concentration between his eyes. She wondered whether he had had a woman since she had left him searching for her in Tunisia. Probably. He was a man of strong sexuality, it would be very hard for him to be without a woman for fifteen months. But if he hadn't—then he must have loved her very much! Lyn gazed unseeingly out of the window, remembering the light kiss he had given her back in her flat, wondering what the day would bring, and how on earth she was going to be able to get through it.

At some point Beric turned off the main road and

drove through a maze of side roads and lanes that seemed to get ever narrower as they headed deeper into the countryside. He didn't need to consult a map, but unerringly drove on until they turned up what was little more than a farm track and after half a mile stopped outside a small, white-painted cottage with a low thatched roof tucked into the fold of a low hill.

Lyn gave a genuine exclamation of delight when she saw it. 'Oh, it's perfect!'

'Worth the drive?'

'Oh, yes.' He came to open her door and Lyn managed to smile at him as she got out. 'I see what you mean about not being able to find my way here if I'd driven down. It really is miles away from anywhere.'

'Yes, I think the nearest house is a farm on the other side of the river over there,' he told her, pointing vaguely to the right. 'And there's no telephone to disturb the peace.'

He led the way up the path through a garden thick with flowers that grew haphazardly: roses among the masses of dahlias and foxgloves poking their heavy heads through a carpet of brilliant pansies. The scent from the garden hung in the still air as Lyn waited for Beric to open the door and she filled her nostrils with it, forgetting for the moment where she was and who she was with. It evoked memories of other gardens, other times. A shadow flickered across her face and for a moment she felt a great sadness in her heart. Why was it that smells always brought back memories so evocatively?

She opened her eyes and came back to reality to find Beric watching her narrowly, a strange look in his blue eyes. Did the scents bring back memories for him, too?

For a moment their glances held, the sadness still in Lyn's face, then he gestured towards the open door and she walked past him into the cottage.

It was very old, the ceilings so low that Beric had to stoop every time he went through a doorway, and there was a beautiful inglenook fireplace in the sitting-room which took up most of the ground floor. There wasn't a lot of furniture, but what there was went well with the house: floral chintz-covered settee and chairs, an old country grandfather clock ticking in the corner, and, in the kitchen, a big scrubbed pine table with ladderback Windsor chairs set round it. Upstairs there were two bedrooms, the larger one with a big brass bed in it, and a tiny bathroom that looked like a fairly new addition.

Beric went round opening windows to let in the fresh air and get rid of the slightly musty smell that old houses get when they've been shut up for some time. Lyn loved the cottage and wished it was hers; it deserved better than to be just used for occasional summer weekends. Beric poured out long drinks and set a couple of chairs out on the little patio at the back of the house which overlooked a sadly overgrown lawn.

'You'll have to cut that before the party, won't you?' Lyn asked, nodding towards the lawn.

'Mmm. There's an electric mower in the shed; it shouldn't take too long. Phew, it's really getting hot!' He'd already taken off his sweater, but now he undid his shirt and pulled it over his head. Lyn took one look at his broad, muscled chest, tanned deep brown from the sun, and hastily looked away, a strange empty feeling in the pit of her stomach. 'Think I'll go and put my shorts on,' he added, then looked at her lazily.

'Why don't you change into your swimsuit?'

'Perhaps later. Is there anything I can do to help get the place ready?'

'Well, if you'd care to cut some flowers, I'm sure it would be appreciated.'

He found her some scissors and a basket and Lyn waded among the blooms, disturbing the butterflies and sending out sprays of seeds from the dead heads. The sun was on her back, burning through the material of her shirt and making her perspire. Her clothes felt thick and uncomfortable, completely wrong. Beric had already changed into his shorts and she could hear the drone of the lawnmower in the back garden. A rose thorn caught at her skirt and pulled a thread. This was silly. She put down the basket and went back into the house, picked up her bag and jacket and took them upstairs to the main bedroom to change into her swimsuit.

Taking off her blouse and skirt, wearing only a slip over her bra and pants, she opened the cupboard built into the wall that served as a wardrobe to look for a spare hanger. There were several items of clothing hanging there, including a pilot's uniform with the four gold rings, but they were all men's clothes, there were no women's clothes at all. Lyn hung her things up and frowned. Surely this Rob Freeman's wife would keep *some* clothes here. That strange cold feeling of fear gripped her again and she quickly turned and began to pull open the drawers of the dresser. Shirts, socks, sweaters—all men's. The fear grew and in a panic she ran to the bedside cabinet, jerked open the top drawer and then froze into stunned immobility. On top of the things in the drawer, as if it had been placed there hurriedly, was a large framed photograph. Of herself.

Taken on their wedding day; standing framed by the doorway of the old church, the white mist of her veil about her blonde head and flowers in her hands. Slowly Lyn reached in and picked up the photograph, stood staring at it, hands trembling, unaware that the sound of the lawnmower had stopped and only birdsong hung on the air.

She didn't hear Beric come up the stairs, only the sound of the latch as he lifted it and came into the room. He stopped on the threshold as he saw her with the photograph in her hands, then deliberately stepped inside and shut the door.

Hastily Lyn dropped the photo frame on the bed, and turned to face him. 'This is *your* cottage,' she said accusingly.

'Yes, that's right.' He came and picked up the photo and put it carefully on the bedside cabinet in a space where it was obvious that it always stood.

'You said it belonged to a friend of yours.'

'Did I?' His mouth twisted mockingly. 'No, I merely said that he was holding the party here.' He gestured towards the photo. 'I see you found the photograph of my wife.'

Her voice little more than a strangled gasp, Lyn said, 'Yes.' Then she yanked open the door of the wardrobe and pulled her clothes out again.

'She's very beautiful, isn't she?'

'Yes.' Lyn pulled her blouse off the hanger and began to put it on.

'What are you doing? I thought you were going to change?'

'Get out of here!' Her voice rose on a high note of fear as he put a hand on her bare shoulder and began to push her blouse off again.

'Not yet.' His head came down as he bent to kiss her neck. 'You know, you remind me so much of her. Of my wife.' He took hold of her blouse from where it was caught round her elbows, pulled it off to drop it in a heap on the floor.

'No! Beric, please!' Lyn tried to push him away, afraid that he would try to make love to her, but he caught her wrists and held them in a vice-like grip.

'You're so much like her,' he repeated softly, 'you could almost be her double.'

'No, I'm nothing like her!' Lyn tried to pull away, but he suddenly jerked her roughly against him. She looked up at him, her eyes filled with fear. There were beads of sweat on his forehead and on his bare, hairy chest. His body was trembling with intense emotion, she could feel it through his hands, and his mouth was drawn back in a thin-lipped snarl. The eyes that glittered down at her were the cold steel-blue of a sword-blade and just as dangerous.

It came to her, sickeningly, that it was fury that was making him shake, not desire; his face was taut with hot, murderous rage that he could hardly control. She realised then, with heart-stopping certainty, that he knew! Had known all along. That there was no party, that he'd made it up in order to trick her into coming down here. He had got her alone, miles from anywhere, and there was no one who could help her!

Realisation must have shown in her face, because his lips twisted into a menacing smile. Lyn screamed in sheer terror, and, fear giving her strength, somehow broke free from his grip and turned to run.

He let her get as far as the head of the stairs before he caught her, forcefully twisting her arm up behind her back, his other hand wound in her hair and pulling so hard that she cried out in pain.

He propelled her back into the bedroom as she struggled vainly, talking in her ear, his voice low and vicious. 'As I was saying, you look very like my wife. The girl who disappeared on our wedding night. Your face is almost the double of hers.' He threw her suddenly face down on to the bed, held her there with one hand pressing her head into the quilt and with his knee across her legs, pinning her down.

Dimly, her face buried in the soft quilt, Lyn heard him say, 'Now let's see how much more like her you are.' And then he caught hold of her slip and tore it violently down to the hem.

Desperately Lyn tried to push herself up with her arms. She managed to scream once, but then he forced her down again.

Almost conversationally he said, 'My wife had a scar on her left hip. Now, wouldn't it be the most fantastic coincidence if you had one there too?' And then his hand was on her pants, jerking them roughly down.

Lyn gave a moan of sheer terror, muffled by the quilt. For a moment the hand on her head tightened, then relaxed as, with his other hand, he touched the scar, slowly tracing the outline of it with his finger. Even in her fear, Lyn could realise what it must mean to him; although he had obviously seen through her, it must still come as a shock to see the proof of his suspicions, to know without any doubt that the woman he loved had played the most cruel trick imaginable on him, had lied and cheated from the very first.

Fear giving her a sudden surge of strength, Lyn took advantage of his absorption to throw herself convulsively sideways off the bed, pulling up her pants as she did so. Then she tried to run for the door, but Beric took one gigantic leap over the bed and pushed her back against the wall.

She cowered back, too frightened to be hurt, putting her hands up in a feeble gesture of defence.

He towered over her, the bitter fury plain in his face. 'So now we know, don't we?' he snarled. 'You bitch! You beautiful, lying bitch!' He gripped her shoulders fiercely, shook her fiercely. 'I could kill you for what you did! Do you hear me?' His voice rose furiously and he let go of her shoulders to move his hands up to her throat. 'I could wring your lovely neck for what you did to me!'

Lyn moaned, too paralysed with fear to move. She felt his fingers tighten round her throat, begin to squeeze. She looked into the murderous rage in his eyes, and then sickening waves of blackness merged into each other as she collapsed unconscious at his feet.

CHAPTER EIGHT

SOMETHING cold and wet splashed her face, ran into her hair and on to her eyelids. Lyn stirred and blinked, automatically putting up a hand to wipe the water from her eyes. She was lying on the bed and Beric was standing over her, watching her, his eyes ice-cold and cruel.

'Oh, no! Oh, God no!' It was more a moan of despair than a prayer. She put her hands up to her throat, felt the tender places where his fingers had pressed. Tears came to her eyes and mingled with the water he had thrown on her.

He sat down suddenly on the edge of the bed. 'How did you do it? How?' Lyn tried to squirm away from him, but he caught her wrists and held them against the pillows, one each side of her head. 'Answer me, you lying bitch! How did you do it?'

For a moment she stared up into his face, dark with unsuppressed fury, then turned her head away, her whole body trembling with the worst fear she had ever known in her life. Stumblingly she answered, 'I—I had an operation on my nose and—and dyed my hair so that you wouldn't recognise me. And I wore coloured contact lenses.'

Beric shook his head with angry impatience. 'That's perfectly obvious. What I want to know is how you managed to disappear so completely in Tunisia.'

Her breath shuddering in her chest, almost choked with fear, and only the greater fear of what he might do to her if she didn't answer driving her on, she managed to stammer, 'I didn't go to the health farm. Instead I went to Tunisia under my own name. With—with a package tour. To the same hotel. Then I said I was going on one of those mini-safaris into the desert for a few days, but instead I . . .' She broke off, realising that what she was going to say would only provoke him further.

But his grip on her wrists tightened, she could feel his fingers right through to her bones. 'Go on,' he commanded bitingly. 'Then what did you do?'

'I went back to England for—for the wedding,' she got out hoarsely, not daring to look him in the face.

'So that was it!' His eyes widened in enlightenment. 'And when you got back to Tunisia with me all you had to do was to walk along to your room and put on whatever disguise you'd been wearing. No one—the police or anybody—would ever think to look for a missing girl among people who'd already been in Tunisia for over a week. How clever! How *bloody* clever!' He glared down at her, his mouth twisted in remembered pain. 'And those last two times, when you phoned me at the hotel and said you'd been kidnapped, and when you called my name at the market, they were easy for you; I only had to hear your voice, not see you at all. And you couldn't let such an easy opportunity go by, could you? You had to stab, and stab again, to make sure that the wound was mortal! And while I was going mad with worry you were probably sunbathing by the hotel pool and laughing your head off. My God, you sadistic little bitch!'

Lyn gave a whimper of terror as his face changed, became venomous with rage. She tried to get away, but he pulled her roughly back.

'Let me go! Please let me go. You're hurting me!'

'Hurting you?' His mouth twisted with satisfaction. 'Good. But this is only a small sample of what you've got coming to you. I intend to make you pay for what you did to me, you callous she-devil. Pay and keep on paying until I've finished with you. And that isn't all you owe me.' His eyes left her face and travelled down her almost naked body, then he pulled her wrists together, took hold of them both in his left hand so that his right was free, free to cup her chin, then slowly move over the smooth whiteness of her shoulder and on down to her breast.

'No! Oh, no, please!' Lyn cried out in despair as he pulled her towards him so that he could reach behind her and unhook her bra.

His voice acid with mocking cruelty, Beric said, 'Why, darling, what's the matter? Have you forgotten that we're married?' He jerked the bra off suddenly and held her arms down so that he could look at her. Lyn turned her head away, helpless tears running down her cheeks. Then she felt his hand, burning hot against her skin, as he began to caress her.

'You owe me our wedding night,' he gritted out, his voice beginning to thicken with desire. 'And you owe me for the months of hell you put me through!'

His hand moved on down the smooth slenderness of her body and Lyn began to shake convulsively, her breath gasping through her dry throat. No! Oh, please God no. Please, God, don't let this be happening to me! The words screamed in her brain, the only coherent thought in her feverish terror and despair. But she'd prayed like that before and still they'd sentenced her, sentenced her to three years!

Anger suddenly exploded through her brain, driving

out every other emotion. Her legs jack-knifed up, kicked out at Beric so that he had to hastily let go of her wrists to stop himself falling on the floor. But instead of making for the door, she turned on him, kneeling on the bed and raining blows on his chest and head with her clenched fists.

'Damn you!' she yelled at him furiously. 'You rotten swine! It was *you* who taught me to lie and cheat. It was your greed and deceit that drove me to it! You deserved everything I did to you—and more, and more!'

Beric put up an arm to protect himself from her fists, then rolled off the bed and stood up, staring at her.

He opened his mouth to speak, but Lyn, her face white with rage, shouted, 'You took three years of my life! You took my name, my home and my parents. You left me with nothing! Nothing but hate. Every day that I was in that terrible prison my hatred for you grew, grew and festered. Planning what I was going to do to you was the only thing that kept me sane. And you deserved it all, everything, for planting that dope on me. Do you hear me? You deserved it all!'

She glared up into his chalk-white face, and then suddenly the fury evaporated and she began to cry again. She became aware of her naked breasts and put her arms up to cover them, bent low over her knees, weeping violently.

Beric stared down at her for several minutes, his face very pale, jaw clenched tight. Then he seemed to come to a decision. Crossing to the wardrobe, he took out some clothes and quickly dressed.

'Lyn.'

She gave a start of fear as he touched her shoulder, and cringed away.

Harshly he said, 'Get dressed. I'll wait for you downstairs.'

It was several minutes before she fully realised that she was alone. Her body still racked by sobs, she at length dragged herself to her feet and began to dress, too numb to wonder why he had left her, only thankful that for the moment his rage had died down. Going into the bathroom, she washed her face in cold water and felt a little better, but there were still dark circles of fear and despair around her eyes. She didn't attempt to put any make-up on to hide them, her hands were shaking too much, and anyway she was sure that Beric hadn't finished with her yet. He hadn't brought her down here like this to let her off so easily. Numbly she combed her hair a little, then, still shaking, she turned to go downstairs and face him again.

He was waiting for her in the sitting-room, a cigarette between his lips and a nearly empty glass in his hand. He looked up swiftly when she came in, his eyes studying her face intently. From somewhere Lyn found the courage to lift her chin and return his look defiantly, but when his eyes narrowed she dropped her head, cowed and beaten.

'Sit down,' he ordered grimly, and after she had obeyed handed her a glass. 'Here, drink this.'

He refilled his own glass as she sipped at the drink. It was brandy. It stung her throat, but she felt better after she'd got some down.

Beric watched her broodingly for a few moments, then ground out his cigarette and threw it in the fireplace. Flatly, his voice sounding very weary, he said, 'You were wrong, Lyn. From the time it happened right up to today. I told you then and I'll tell you again now: I wasn't the one who planted the dope on you.'

Lyn looked up, open disbelief in her eyes.

'Believe me or not, what difference does it make now? But at least I learnt something today.' He waited for her to speak, but when she didn't he went on heavily, 'I learnt that you *really believed* I'd framed you. I couldn't credit that at the time; I thought you were just trying to pin the thing on to me because you'd done it yourself and were getting desperate. And that's what turned my stomach, made me so disgusted that I walked out on you.'

'What are you saying?' Lyn got to her feet and faced him. 'Are you still trying to wriggle out of it? Still trying to pin the blame on someone else? It was *you*. I know it was you!'

'No.' He said it very quietly and calmly, shaking his head. His blue eyes regarded her steadily, filled with what Lyn recognised with a shock as pity.

She stared at him, more shaken by that one word uttered so quietly than she would have been by long arguments or shouted denials.

'But—but you must be! You've *got* to be,' she said wildly, her voice rising. 'Are you trying to tell me that all those years in prison . . . everything I did to you . . . No!' She rounded on him, close to hysteria. 'No, I don't believe it! I *won't* believe it! You're lying again.'

Taking a quick step across the room, Beric caught hold of her shoulders and turned her to face him. 'Lyn! Look at me. Look at me!' he ordered again, putting a hand under her chin and forcing her to obey him. 'I'm not lying. I don't have to lie—because I *know* I didn't do it. And now,' his voice changed, 'God help me, I know you didn't do it either.'

Her own eyes wide in her pale face, Lyn stared up at

him, trying to read his face, looking for the slightest
sign of wavering in the blue eyes that looked down at
her so steadily. After a long, long moment she looked
away, shaking her head.

'It's been too long. I've hated you for too long for
me to believe you now.'

After a moment he let her go and went to lean against
the inglenook, lighting another cigarette and drawing
on it deeply before he spoke again.

'All right,' he said eventually, 'so you don't believe
me. But you're at least going to give me the chance to
prove it to you.'

His tone was very decisive, making Lyn look at him
sharply. 'What do you mean?'

'I mean that we're going to go back and find out
who *did* plant it on you. We'll start with the crew and
go on through every passenger who was on the plane,
if we have to.'

Lyn's eyes widened in amazement. 'You're crazy!
You'd never find out anything after all this time. It's
been nearly five years. And anyway, what's the point?
If it wasn't you as you say, then why should you want
to bother to find out who really did it?'

Beric took his cigarette from his mouth, looked at it
as if he found it suddenly distasteful. Grimly he
answered, 'You hurt me once. If I don't prove my innocence to you, what's to stop you hurting me again?'

Bereft of words, Lyn could only gaze at him, then
she turned agitatedly away. 'You said we—we would
find out who did it.' She swung round to face him, her
voice scornful. 'What makes you think that I'd have
anything to do with this wild goose chase?'

He smiled thinly. 'You're going to whether you want
to or not. I'm not letting you out of my sight until

we've got this thing sorted out.'

Her chin came up defiantly. 'And if I refuse?'

His voice silky, Beric answered, 'Then I'm sure the police would be very interested to know that you had two passports, and where you got the second one from in the name of Netta Lewis. Especially with your record,' he added deliberately.

For the second time Lyn was unable to speak. She turned away and walked over to the window, looking unseeingly out into the sunlit garden. Bitterly she blamed herself for giving him a weapon to hold over her head. Even if she ran away again she wouldn't be able to leave the country without first getting another false passport; not with her name blacklisted in every port and airport. Not that there was much chance of running away; she had no illusions about that. Beric would stick to her like glue now that he'd found her again.

She tried to think what his new tack of questioning the crew and the passengers could mean, what was behind it. Did he plan to get his revenge by some means she couldn't begin to fathom? Or was he telling the truth? Had done so all along? But no, it couldn't be that. Her mind shrank away from the possibility. That would be worse to bear than all the rest. She couldn't live with the knowledge of what she'd done to him, if he was innocent.

She pondered the problem for some time, but then something else occurred to her and she said, 'How did you know it was me? I mean, how did you know that Netta Lewis and I were the same person? When did you guess the truth?' She turned to look at him as she spoke and found him watching her closely. He wasn't so pale any more and she noticed that the dejected look had gone from his eyes and around his mouth.

He gave a grim sort of smile. 'I knew from the first moment that I saw you, on the plane.'

Lyn's eyes widened in amazement. 'But you gave no sign.'

'No.' His voice grew harsh. 'I've had plenty of time to learn how to hide my feelings. And if I'd let you see I'd have lost you again. I had to let you think I believed you so that you'd feel secure for a while, and I'd have time to go to my flat and get the keys of the cottage.'

'I see. You hid it very well. But you still haven't told me how you recognised me.'

His mouth twisted sardonically. 'You don't forget someone you love. They're there with you, all the time, alive in your mind and your heart. I remembered every detail about you: the softness of your skin, the way you tilted your head to look at me, your mouth when you smiled, your voice, and the frightened look you sometimes had in your eyes when you thought you weren't being watched. They were all there, the first moment I saw you. And later there was the way you walked and held a glass, the clean, sweet smell of your hair. No matter where or when, I would always have known you,' he finished simply.

'But you didn't recognise me in Singapore,' she reminded him.

'No, because it had been three years, and because I'd deliberately shut you out of my mind. But maybe even then, in my subconscious, I knew who you were.'

A choking sensation filled Lyn's chest and she had to turn quickly away, feeling suddenly ashamed, and afraid that he would see.

After a pause in which she tried to recover herself,

she said huskily. 'What do you want me to do?'

Promptly he answered, 'First I want your word that you won't try to run away again.'

Lyn turned to him in surprise. 'My word? But even if I gave it to you, how could you possibly believe it after what I've done to you?'

A shadow passed over his eyes, but he said firmly, 'I'd believe it.'

'Why?'

'Because if I'd been in your shoes—if I'd believed that someone had deliberately framed me and put me in prison—then maybe I'd have done the same thing.'

Beric's eyes met hers quite steadily as he spoke, and Lyn could only stare back in stunned surprise. Then she bit her lip and looked away, afraid to think the thing through, afraid of her own conscience. 'All right,' she agreed at length, 'I give you my word.'

'Good. Then let's work out what we're going to do.'

His tone was brisk and he kept it that way as they sat down and discussed all round the subject—Beric, without actually saying it, assuming that she was now giving him the benefit of the doubt, and Lyn tacitly accepting the situation, but never letting her defences down.

'We'll start with the crew,' he told her, 'because they'll be easier to trace. And first we'll go and talk to the other stewardesses.' Seeing her raised eyebrows, he explained, 'It always bothered me that the dope was hidden in a carton of talcum powder of a brand that only women used. If the Customs had done just an ordinary check they might have noticed it was out of place in a man's baggage and decided to investigate further, so for the moment we'll assume that a woman planted it on you.' He paused, but when she didn't have any argument, went on, 'Now I suggest that I go to the airline offices on Monday and get the present addresses of the stewardesses from the personnel files.'

'Will they give them to you?' Lyn asked dubiously.

He grinned without humour. 'There's a girl who works in the department who's persuadable.'

Lyn glanced at him swiftly. Of course, he still had all the old charm, was still handsome and masculine enough to attract any woman; she'd forgotten that. A fierce stab of emotion filled her and she looked away.

'It will take time to interview all these people,' she pointed out.

'I'll get it,' he assured her. Adding with heavy irony, 'I'll tell the airline that I've had news of my wife and I have to follow it up. They're very sympathetic. They'll give me the time off, just like they gave me time off when you disappeared.'

'They did?' Somehow Lyn felt compelled to ask.

'Yes,' he answered grimly. 'Six futile months that I spent searching for you in North Africa.'

'It's useless. We're just wasting our time.'

Lyn was sitting in Beric's car a few days later outside a block of luxury flats in the most expensive part of Mayfair. They had just been to see one of the stewardesses who had been on the plane with them the day Lyn was arrested. The girl no longer worked for the airline and had since married. Beric had been optimistic when they saw the address, thinking that her lifestyle might indicate that she was living on money gained from drug smuggling, but it had turned out that she had married a very rich man who was well able to provide everything she wanted. She had also been very sympathetic, offering to do anything she could to help them: have her fingerprints taken, submit to a drugs test, anything. And Lyn had come away feeling sick with humiliation.

'What's the point of going on?' she demanded angrily. 'No one's going to come right out and tell us they did it. We're just raking it all up again for nothing.'

'No, we're not,' Beric retorted firmly. 'We've eliminated three people already. There are only two more stewardesses to see.'

'Yes, and one of them lives in Australia now. Are you going all the way there to talk to her?'

'Yes, if I have to!' Beric snapped back. 'Don't be so damn defeatist. Isn't proving your innocence worth a fight?'

Lyn bit her lip. 'I'm—I'm sorry,' she said huskily. 'It isn't easy seeing them all again, knowing what they must think.'

'Then the sooner we get it over the better. Now, where does the next one live? What's her name—Susan Saunders.'

'In Hertfordshire. A place called Garston, near Watford. Only she's married now, too, and her name's Warner.' She shook her head. 'I can't remember her at all, can you?'

'No.' Beric started up the car. 'There's a London area road map in the back. It shouldn't take us more than an hour or so to get there.'

But traffic held them up and they stopped for lunch on the way so that it was early afternoon before they drew up in front of a nondescript, neglected-looking council house in the sprawling suburb. Lyn looked at the place in surprise and checked the address again before getting out of the car. Immediately the sun beat

down on her bare head. It had been cool in the car
with the air-conditioning on and the roof open, but
even in the sleeveless sundress she was wearing it still
felt stifling, the heat coming up from the pavement in
waves.

'It doesn't look very prepossessing,' she remarked as
Beric joined her. 'Anybody who'd made the sort of
money you get from drug smuggling wouldn't end up
in a place like this.'

'Not unless they were on to drugs themselves.' He
gripped her elbow and she could feel his inner excitement. 'Come on.'

They pushed aside the broken gate and walked up
the path between what had once been pocket-sized
lawns but which were now overgrown with weeds, a
rusted, broken tricycle and other children's playthings
left rotting in the grass.

There was no bell, so Beric hammered on the door.
Immediately the high whine of a child and the sound
of a dog barking came from the other side. A woman
shouted for quiet, but neither took any notice of her
and both child and dog were still loudly making their
presence felt when she opened the door.

'Yes?' The woman, unmade-up, her hair lank and
untidy, dressed in stained jeans and faded blouse,
carried the squalling baby on her hip while with her
other hand she tried to restrain the dog.

Lyn recognised her then, but only just, as the girl
she'd worked alongside on that last flight, looking after
the passengers at the back of the plane. But then she'd
been slim and well-groomed, her face pretty. But now
. . . Lyn could hardly credit the degeneration.

The woman's eyes went impassively over Lyn as she
tried to soothe the baby, but they widened in first re-

cognition and then horror as she looked at Beric and then quickly back at Lyn. Colour drained from her face and she sagged against the door jamb, almost dropping the baby. Fear, terror and guilt chased across her face, and then she made a movement to close the door, but Beric leapt up the step and shouldered it open. 'We want a word with you, Mrs Warner,' he said grimly.

Lyn followed numbly, and found Beric confronting the girl in a dirty kitchen that smelled of dog and babies. There was another man there too, a pallid-faced, bearded man who sat in a wheelchair with another child not much bigger than the first on his lap. He looked at Lyn as she came in, but his eyes were empty, apathetic.

Susan Warner was crying, her hand to her face. 'Oh God, I knew you'd come. I knew one day they'd find out.'

'We want the truth, all of it!' Beric shouted harshly above the noisy sound of her weeping. 'Either here or at the police station.'

'I had to do it. It was Steve.' Agitatedly she pointed to the man in the wheelchair. 'He—he'd got hooked and—and they blackmailed him. Said if he didn't get me to bring the stuff in for them, they'd—they'd . . .' Her words were broken off by more bitter sobs, but at least the child had stopped, it just sat and gazed up at her with large wet eyes. She gulped and went on, 'They said they'd beat him up and wouldn't let him have any more drugs.'

'But you weren't married to him then,' Beric pointed out.

'No, but we were—we were living together.'

Lyn stood just inside the door, watching wordlessly

as Beric drew it all out of her. The number of times she'd done it, her panic on that particular day when she'd been given a last-minute tip-off about the search waiting for her in London. 'I didn't know what to do,' she told him. 'Then—then I saw her,' she nodded towards Lyn, 'drop her bag at Miami Airport and everybody help to pick the things up. And I realised that if I put the powder carton in her bag it wouldn't matter. If my fingerprints were found on it I could just say that I picked it up for her. So—so when she left her bag while she saw to a passenger I put the stuff in there.'

The words seared into Lyn's brain, but somehow she felt too numb to react, she felt completely drained of emotion, she couldn't even feel angry or bitter as the woman spilled out her pitiful story, the words tumbling over each other now as if she was glad to say them, glad to confess her guilt at last. Beric made her put the child down while she sat at a table and wrote it all out and signed the confession.

Then he straightened, the statement in his hands. 'You realise that we'll go straight to the police with this?'

'Yes.' The former stewardess nodded hopelessly. 'I won't try to deny it. I'm glad it's come out. I've had to live with it for too long.' She lifted her eyes reluctantly to Lyn's face, tried to say something, then looked away again, fresh sobs racking her body. 'My kids—what will happen to my kids?'

Beric nodded towards the man in the wheelchair who had sat silently throughout the whole thing. 'This is your husband?' And when she nodded, added, 'How did he get like that?'

Her voice not much more than a whisper, Susan

Warner answered dully, 'He was high on drugs. He took the car and smashed it into a wall. He can't walk any more.'

Beric nodded, then turned to Lyn. 'I think we've got all we want.' Repugnance showed in his face. 'Let's get out of here. Lyn!' he said sharply when she didn't move.

A shudder ran through her and she blinked as if she'd just come awake. Slowly she held out her hand for the confession and after a moment's hesitation he gave it to her. She looked at it for a long moment, seeing the unsteady signature, the tear blotches, seeing there the long-dreamed-of proof of her innocence. She crossed to the table and looked down at the bowed head of the girl who had ruined her life, waited until she looked up and their eyes met. Then Lyn deliberately tore the paper through and through again. 'Burn it,' she said shortly. 'You don't have to be afraid; you won't hear from us again, and we won't go to the police.' Then she turned quickly and walked past Beric, out of the kitchen and the dingy house and into the open sunlight again.

Silently Beric joined her in the car and drove quickly away, heading into the open countryside. He looked at her several times, but Lyn gazed straight ahead, her face set, hands gripped together in her lap. After about twenty minutes or so he pulled off the lane into the entrance to a field near some woods and switched off the engine.

He wound down the window and the sound of crickets in the long grass filled the quiet of the afternoon. 'That was quite something you did back there,' he remarked.

Lyn looked down at her hands. 'She'd made a far

worse prison for herself than any with cells and bars. And what good would it have done? It couldn't have given me back the years I've lost. Or what you've lost.' Abruptly she pushed open the door of the car, got out and began to run across the field towards the woods, the grass soft and springy under her feet. It was cooler under the shade of the trees and there were flowers growing among the bracken, but she kept on running, not stopping until she reached a clearing where the sun dappled down through the tree tops. It was very still and quiet, only the distant birdsong high on the summer air. The grass was very green, spattered with flowers, where butterflies, their wings spread like jewels in the sunlight, came to settle.

Lyn stood there breathless, not really seeing where she was, her arms clasped together as if she was very cold. She heard Beric coming after her and she looked up. He stopped precipitately on the edge of the glade, then slowly moved forward into the sunlight, watching her guardedly.

'I'm sorry,' she burst out. 'Oh God, I'm sorry.' Then she turned away, biting her lip, her hands digging hard into her arms. 'Oh, what a stupid thing to say. What a damn stupid word! As if it could possibly make any difference after what I did to you.'

'No, it couldn't,' he agreed. 'But maybe straight answers to some questions might.'

His tone more than his words gave Lyn the courage to turn round and look at him. He was standing in a patch of sunlight, the rays slanting down on to his already tanned skin, shadowed where the lines of unhappiness drew in his mouth.

In little more than a whisper, she said, 'What questions?'

The guarded look was still in his eyes and for a moment he hesitated, as if unsure of himself, but then his jaw tightened and he said abruptly, 'That first time, before you went to prison, you said that you loved me. Did you mean it?'

Lyn reached up and pulled a leaf from a low-hanging branch, looked down at it blindly. 'Yes,' she answered softly, then looked at him. 'If I hadn't loved you I'd never have been able to hate you so much.'

A muscle jerked in his jaw, but Beric went on, 'And the second time; was it all just hate?'

With nervous fingers Lyn began to pull the leaf apart. 'Yes, I hated you.' Then suddenly she threw it down and stood erect. 'But I hated myself for what I was doing even more. All the time I had to keep on telling myself how much I hated you. Because if I hadn't ... If I hadn't ...' Tears poured down her cheeks and she couldn't go on. Her body crumpled as she put her hands up to cover her face, turning away from him.

But then Beric's hands were on her shoulders, making her turn to face him. Roughly he pulled her hands down and said forcefully, 'And now? And now, Lyn?'

She stared up at him through her tears, saw the urgency in his face but with emotion still held in check. 'I love you,' she whispered. 'Oh God, I love you so much!'

He gave a great sigh, as if he'd been holding his breath, and his face relaxed, lost its tenseness. He pulled her hard against him, held her very tightly, as if he was trying to weld her body into his, make her a part of him so that he would never lose her again.

Lyn put her arms round his waist and pressed herself

against him, glad of the crushing strength of his arms, of the hard muscles that bruised her skin. Her face was buried in the open neck of his shirt and she could smell the tangy scent of his after-shave and feel the soft dew of perspiration on his skin. For a long time they just held one another, overwhelmed by their need for the reassurance of their closeness, both of them trembling with emotion. But then Lyn looked up, the tears still wet on her face.

'How can you forgive me? How can you possibly forgive me?'

'Forget it,' he said roughly. 'It's over.'

'But *you* won't be able to forget.'

'Perhaps not entirely. But all I need to remember is that life isn't worth very much without you. So you're stuck with me, like it or not.'

He reached up a hand to either side of her face, his eyes gazing into hers with silent intensity. Then he bent and kissed her, his lips hard and bruising. It wasn't a sexual kiss, more a communication of need and love and forgiveness, a means of wiping away the past and starting anew. And when at last he let her go there was a new brilliance in his eyes. 'Oh, my darling, if you only knew how much I love you!'

'Beric.' Lyn put her arms round his neck, ran her fingers in his hair. 'We've wasted so much time, lost so many years.' She stood on tiptoe to kiss him, her lips hungry for the feel of his mouth, and this time their embrace was sensuous, passionate, her lips opening under his as she moved against him, her insides on fire and her only thought to convince him of her love. He returned the kiss with savage abandon, his fingers hurting her as he held her against the lean length of his body.

Abruptly he moved his head away and Lyn could feel his heart hammering in his chest. His voice thick, uncontrolled, he said, 'Lyn! Oh, God, darling, I need you so much. And I've waited so long, so long. I want you now, Lyn, *now!*'

'Here?' Lyn pulled away from him a little. 'Oh, but . . .' The words of protest died on her lips as she looked into his face. Slowly she reached up to touch the tortured lines by his mouth, then she looked round the sunstrewn glade and knew that it was right. Here in the clean, open air they could wash away all the hurt and malice of the past. Gently she moved out of his arms and slipped the straps of her dress off her shoulders, let it fall to the ground, then slowly took off the rest of her clothes.

Beric watched her as though transfixed, his body shaking with anticipation, beads of perspiration on his brow and growing wonder in his face. For a moment neither of them moved, then Lyn held out her arms and he lunged for her, picking her up in his arms and kissing her lips, her throat, her breasts, saying her name over and over again. Then he carried her to a patch of sunlight under the spreading branches of a tree and laid her gently down on the soft green grass. Tenderly he stroked her hair, spreading it about her head in a glowing aureole, his eyes warm, caressing, as he feasted them on her face, but then they grew dark with passion and desire as his hands wandered down, exploring, fondling.

He tried to be gentle, the first time, but his need was so great and Lyn's response so sensual that he lost control and gentleness vanished as he took her in a blaze of savage rapture. Their mingled cries echoed through the wood and Lyn moaned as she felt his body galvanise with excitement. For a while then they lay in each other's arms, but for Beric the waiting had been hard and long, and soon he was kissing her again, his hands rousing her to a wild frenzy, and this time their lovemaking was mutually ecstatic, mutually fulfilled. His need of her convinced Lyn that there was nothing to fear, the past was dead and buried, and the love he gave her, with no word of blame or censure, made her feel infinitely humble. She didn't deserve such love, such generous forgiveness, but gladly in her heart she accepted it. And now, in the dappled glade, she lost herself in the inflamed abandon of his embrace and gloried in the giving of her body, again and again, to the man she loved.

It was almost dusk when they went back to the car. Beric drove slowly with Lyn leaning her head against his shoulder. She had one hand on his arm, the other on his knee, wanting still to be as near to him as she could, to feel the wonder of his physical presence close to her. Her face glowed with rapture, still amazed and thrilled that they belonged to each other, that her lover was near, could be seen, heard, touched.

Beric looked at her and smiled, his hand coming down to cover hers. Then he drew up outside a small hotel, a low building with a thatched roof and ivy climbing up the walls, a flower-edged stream running through the garden. 'This looks a good place.'

Lyn sat up. 'For dinner?'

He grinned and kissed her possessively. 'For a honeymoon.'

She laughed, but then a thought occurred to her and she looked at him questioningly. 'But are we—really married, I mean?'

'Why shouldn't we be?'

'Well—I did give a false name.'

Beric pursed his lips. 'I should think so. We were both physically present, and were married in the sight of man.' He turned his head towards her, said softly, 'And now in the sight of God.'

Lyn blushed, answered huskily, 'Yes.'

They got out of the car and she stood waiting while he locked it, but hesitated as he turned to go in. 'What will we tell your parents, other people, when you turn up with a wife with a different name and appearance?'

Beric shrugged. 'What's wrong with the truth? Or we could make up some story to explain it away; say I'd had the first marriage annulled and you're my second wife or something. Does it matter?'

She looked at him, saw joy and thankfulness in his eyes, and new contentment and happiness in his face, replacing the lines of bitterness and torment which were already beginning to fade. She shook her head. 'No, nothing matters so long as we're together.'

Then she put her hand in his and let him lead her into the first day of their future.

A LOVE STORY OF LONG AGO

The literally rags-to-riches story of Nell Gwyn has been a favorite of British storytellers for more than three hundred years. What follows is a sketch of that tale—all we have room for!—but perhaps you will be intrigued enough to research this fascinating historical figure on your own.

"Pretty, witty Nell," as she came to be called by all whose lives she touched, was a child of the slums, poverty forcing her to sell oranges and, by the time she was fourteen, herself. But soon she left the streets behind and took up a career as a stage actress.

It was at the age of seventeen that she caught the fancy of Britain's dashing King Charles II—noted for his extravagances, self-indulgence... and his many love affairs. The King was utterly charmed by Nell's high spirits and exquisite beauty, and it wasn't long before she became his mistress; since any mistress of the King was highly regarded, she, and the two sons she eventually bore him, were well provided for. She was adored by courtiers and the poor alike, for what distinguished her from the King's other inamoratas was her sharp wit, kind nature and generous heart.

That the King loved her in his way, there is no doubt; that she loved him is proven by her faithfulness to him for seventeen years, until his death in 1685.

Readers all over the country say Harlequin is the best!

"You're #1."

A.H.*, Hattiesburg, Missouri

"Harlequin is the best in romantic reading."

K.G., Philadelphia, Pennsylvania

"I find Harlequins are the only stories on the market that give me a satisfying romance, with sufficient depth without being maudlin."

C.S., Bangor, Maine

"Keep them coming! They are still the best books."

R.W., Jersey City, New Jersey

*Names available on request.

FREE!

A hardcover Romance Treasury volume
containing 3 treasured works of romance
by 3 outstanding Harlequin authors...

...as your introduction to Harlequin's
Romance Treasury subscription plan!

Romance Treasury

...almost 600 pages of exciting romance reading
every month at the low cost of $6.97 a volume!

A wonderful way to collect many of Harlequin's most beautiful love
stories, all originally published in the late '60s and early '70s.
Each value-packed volume, bound in a distinctive gold-embossed
leatherette case and wrapped in a colorfully illustrated dust jacket,
contains...
- 3 full-length novels by 3 world-famous authors of romance fiction
- a unique illustration for every novel
- the elegant touch of a delicate bound-in ribbon bookmark...
  and much, much more!

Romance Treasury

...for a library of romance you'll treasure forever!

Complete and mail today the FREE gift certificate and subscription
reservation on the following page.

Romance Treasury

An exciting opportunity to collect treasured works of romance! Almost 600 pages of exciting romance reading in each beautifully bound hardcover volume!

You may cancel your subscription whenever you wish! You don't have to buy any minimum number of volumes. Whenever you decide to stop your subscription just drop us a line and we'll cancel all further shipments.